Ill Fated

A Maurin Kincaide Novel

Rachel Rawlings

Ill fated

A Maurin Kincaide Novel

Written by Rachel Rawlings

Copyright © 2015 Rachel Rawlings

Published in the United States by: R Squared Publishing

http://www.rachelrawlings.com http://www.hallowread.com

Dedication

This book is dedicated to my family. To my husband and three amazing children who put up with my poor time management skills. Thank you for your love and understanding, for supporting me when despite the long hours. Thank you for helping me live my dream.

Thank you to Karmin Dahl, my editor. You really came through in a pinch and I am eternally grateful.

To Stephanie, my first reader and dear friend. And to Gladys, my biggest champion and cheerleader.

No one should be awake at four in the morning. Especially me. I ripped the plug for my alarm clock out of the wall around three-thirty.

I forgot about the batteries.

The numbers on the clock taunted me like a green-eyed devil until I finally got out of bed. I fumbled in the dark to make a pot of coffee, refusing to turn on the kitchen light and formally acknowledge the day. I pulled my favorite mug out of the cabinet and filled it before settling at my table.

The dream came every night - technically morning - at three o'clock. I was used to running on little-to-no sleep, this bordered on ridiculous. Yesterday at the range I shot a target in the lane on my left. Fortunately, it had been Mason's and I played everything off by exaggerating my sharp-shooting skills. Someone else could have had me banned. As it was, Mason thought I was being a competitive brat.

I wasn't sure I preferred that to being a sleep-deprived danger to others.

I scratched my neck, pausing when I felt the delicate silver chain. I followed it down to the apple branch charm which rested on my chest. Weird. I could have sworn I took it off last night. I slid the charm back and forth as I went over the dream. Again.

After the first week, I'd broken down and started analyzing it. According to Freud, I had mommy issues. No surprise there. I seriously doubted my relationship - or lack thereof - with my adoptive mother was the cause of the recurring dream.

I fired up the laptop, unwilling to cease my search for answers. Instead of the trippy New Age sites I checked out last night, I went back to my trusty Google. I nodded off twice as I scanned the results.

What the hell did an old woman washing clothes in a river have to do with me? I might have written it off as paranoia or a side effect of all the spicy food I'd been eating, if not for the haggard old woman crooking her bony finger at me and called my name - every time.

I finally got a hit on an obscure mythology website. Bean Nighe, the washer woman of the Highlands. She scrubbed the bloody linens of those doomed to die. Knowing she was fae bothered me more than the knowledge the clothes she washed every night were mine. Impending death I could handle. Hell, I'd slipped through the Reaper's grasp more than once. The Fae on the other hand, well they could be tricky

The phone rang just as I got up for a refill. The fact someone else was not only awake at this ungodly hour, but calling me, meant it was bad news. No one who valued their life called me before noon unless it was an emergency - one of the perks of my new position as Regulator.

I was now in charge of one investigator, two trackers and a team of cleaners. It was a lot like it sounds. We investigate, we track and we clean up. We clean up everything, no loose ends. You don't ever want to find yourself in need of a cleaner. Late hours came with the new job, hence the "no calls before noon" rule.

I glanced at the screen before answering and recognized the number immediately. It helped I had been dialing it for the last four years - it used to belong to Captain Matthison. Of course Mason, my fae boyfriend and member of the Wild Hunt, was the captain of SPTF now.

We'd been officially dating for a couple months, moved well past first base. Hell, I had a key to his apartment. Granted I hadn't used it since the night he gave it to me. I'd been dragging my feet, leaving deep ruts in my wake where our relationship was concerned. My track record wasn't all that great. I'd rushed in before, once because I was spelled and once because I wanted to.

Neither ended well.

Things were going great. I was afraid if I labeled it, changed it in anyway, the change would be catastrophic. Thankfully, Mason was a patient man.

Except when it came to a four a.m. phone call. My phone stopped then immediately started ringing again.

My answer was short and to the point. "Morning."

"You're awake?" He sounded more than a little surprised.

"I'm not really sure the state I'm in qualifies as awake."

"Here I was, terrified to poke the dragon, and you're already drinking coffee and talking in complete sentences."

I snorted and took a sip of the aforementioned liquid gold. "Are you always like this in the morning?"

"If you'd let me sleep over you'd already know the answer to that question. Why aren't you asleep?"

In general or just tonight, I silently wondered. "Bad dream. I've been tossing and turning all night. I finally gave in and got out of bed."

Papers rustled in the background and when he spoke again, his voice was lower, intimate, "You want to talk about it?"

"Something tells me my nightmares are the least of our problems."

"You have no idea. I need you to come down to my office."

I sighed. "Can it at least wait until after sunrise?"

"Would I be breaking the 'no phone calls before noon'policy if it could wait?"

"There really is no rest for the wicked, is there?"

4

He laughed and the sound warmed me more than a hundred cups of coffee. "Apparently not, in your case. Now, there's a dirty chai latte and a croissant for you if you're here before Amalie. I can't promise real coffee and pastries will survive beyond five minutes of her arrival."

"It's four-thirty in the morning, Mas. If you know what's good for you, you'll make sure at *least* one dirty chai and croissant remain unmolested."

"I'll see you soon." He was laughing as he hung up the phone.

Three hours ago, I'd practically crawled through the doorway, exhausted from cleaning up after a newbie vamp who'd broken the Jus Sanguinis Intergentes when she killed her donor. The blood pact between people and vampires had a clear 'no killing, no exceptions' clause.

It was up to the maker to ensure their child was ready to feed unsupervised. If something went wrong and the Council found out about it, we cleaned up the mess and the sire was subject to heavy fines and possible revocation of their rights to expand their blood lines. She'd been quite literally a bitch to track and take down.

It had been a long night and it was shaping up to be an even longer day.

I wasted little time getting dressed, opting for a slip-on black jersey dress, eighteen hole Docs and a leather jacket. Jewelry was a hindrance in my line of work. My meeting with Mason could easily turn into a run. Choked with my own chain? No, thank you. Unclasping the necklace, I set it in a glass dish on my bathroom counter. I ran a brush through my hair, a toothbrush over my teeth and slipped into the Between. I stepped out of the alley two buildings down from the station and walked the last block and a half.

Amalie was swarmed by detectives trying to get at the goodies she brought over from the Daily Grind. She greeted me with a warm smile, shaking her head when I offered to pull her out of the fray. She had managed to endear herself to the entire department in record time. All it took was real coffee and fresh pastries. I pointed to Mason's office. She'd make her way over once the starving masses had their fill.

Mason was so engrossed in the file on his desk he didn't hear me come in. He looked as tired as I felt - too many double shifts. Despite an uptick in activity, SPTF was short-staffed due to budget cuts. Without enough man power to staff the shifts properly, overtime was mandatory.

"Is that for me?" I pointed at the to-go cup and white paper bag on his desk.

He finally looked up and gave me a smile which lit up his whole face. "As promised."

I stole a quick kiss, grabbed the coffee and croissant, and settled in the chair across from him. I took a long sip of my latte, savoring the delicious mix of tea and espresso. "Man, I needed this. Is that the case you're working on?"

"Yeah, we've got a real problem on our hands."

"Don't we always." I tried to peek at the file.

Mason closed the manila folder. "I'd rather wait until everyone is here."

"Who else is coming besides Amalie?" My curiosity was definitely peaked now. I reached across his desk, hoping to grab the file.

"You look exhausted. Tell me about your dream while we wait."

I narrowed my eyes and glared at him. "I see this for the obvious distraction it is." Sighing, I rubbed my temple. "However, I'm exhausted, too exhausted to argue. So I'll tell you. Prepare to be confounded."

He listened intently as I filled him in on the nightly visits from the weathered old woman who washed my clothes and hauntingly called my name. I expected him to laugh and tell me it was just a dream, that I had nothing to worry about.

I didn't expect him to look so stricken.

"Bean Nighe." He whispered the name.

"You've heard of her?"

"Of course I've heard of her. How long has she been coming to you?"

I stared at him curiously. "A few weeks. Why?"

When I agreed to give this thing with Mason a chance I also agreed to some conditions. No more flying solo, no more rash decisions or rushing off to play the hero. We were a team, in everything. This was just one of many setbacks.

"A few weeks and this is the first I'm hearing of it?" He closed his eyes and took a deep breath, obviously struggling to control his temper. "We talked about this. No holding things back, remember?"

"I thought it was just a dream." I shrugged. "Honestly, I didn't think it was a big deal."

"It was a big enough deal for you to research it." Agitation rolled off him in waves.

"I got curious, did a little digging. Until tonight, everything I found pointed to deep-seated family issues, particularly with a mother figure. I've told you about my childhood, does that dream analysis surprise you?"

His growl told me he wasn't in the mood for reasonable explanations. "When did you discover the true meaning of the dream? How long have you known about the Bean Nighe?"

"Tonight. This morning. Before you called me." I held up a hand to stop the tongue lashing I knew he wanted to give me. "I would have told you. I got the impression on the phone there were more pressing matters than my insomnia."

"Is this why you won't let me stay at your place?" His gaze roamed over my face, searching. "Why you never stay at mine?"

"Is that the real reason why you're so upset?" I arched my brows. "Because we're not having sleepovers?"

"I stayed at your lovely apartment the first night we met."

I turned to watch Aidan glide into the room, stopping behind my chair. Rolling my eyes, I snorted and muttered, "In the closet."

Mason's jaw twitched, but he didn't take the bait. "Aidan."

"It's almost sunrise. Shouldn't you be hunkered down for the day?" I sighed, wondering what he was doing here. I was too tired to deal with Aidan and Mason and their combined testosterone.

Putting the three of us in a room together was like throwing lit matches at sticks of dynamite - eventually one of them will explode. So far we'd managed to avoid any real fireworks. Aidan and I have to work together-he's part of my crew and usually all business when we're on the council's time. Get us all together for something other than a case and Aidan couldn't help verbally jabbing Mason.

I knew he still had feelings for me. So did Mason. Vampires tend to hold onto things for a while, even emotions. So for now, we did our best to ignore it.

The look on Mason's face said this time he was not going to be able to rise above it.

"Mason requested my presence. Apparently, he is in need of my help with a case."

I didn't have to turn around to see the smug look on Aidan's face. I knew he enjoyed the role reversal. Not too long ago, Mason had been brought in to train me on the finer points of moving and tracking in the Between- things Aidan couldn't help me with. Mason did more than train me, he was the final nail in the coffin of my relationship with Aidan. And now he was forced to ask for Aidan's help. My vampire ex was no doubt eating it up.

"Or is it in the bedroom? Is our feisty fae proving to be too much for you?" He leaned in, his lips close to my ear as he whispered, "Ménage a trois?"

Mason white-knuckled the arms of his chair. He looked ready to rip one of the wooden armrests off and stab Aidan in the chest with it.

"Whew, I didn't think I'd make it out of that mob with all my body parts intact." Amalie must have sensed the tension from out in the pit - the area where all the detectives sat. She would have come in even if doing so cost her an arm.

Mason cleared his throat, fully aware Amalie stopped a potential battle with only her smile and bubbly personality. "Now that we're all here, let's get started. We don't have much time." He nodded toward Aidan before leveling his gaze on me. "We think there's a bounty on your head."

The testosterone-fueled tension in the room evaporated. Power laced with fear quickly replaced it as everyone in the room absorbed what he said. One of our own was under attack.

Me.

"What? Why didn't you tell me that as soon as I got here?" I'd had people gunning for me before. Goddess knows I've pissed off my fair share of people. Still, none of them would offer a reward for my head. None who were still alive or living this side of Faerie, that is.

Mason was obviously frustrated. He wasn't just the captain of SPTF, he was part of the Hunt and someone had put a bounty on his girlfriend's head. He shoved the file on his desk-my file, I realized-away. "We picked this guy up outside of Toil and Trouble. Mike gave us a call after tossing him out for fighting. The brawl continued in the parking lot. By the time the first officers arrived on the scene, he was the only one standing."

Leaning back in his chair, Mason rubbed the nape of his neck. "Guy must have figured we were some small town department and tried to run. Took a few shots from the riot gun and a silver bullet clean through the Achilles tendon before my officers took him down. They found a picture of you in his back pocket and a small arsenal in the saddle bags on his bike."

Aidan squeezed my shoulder. Grateful for the comforting gesture, my hand slid over his. Aidan's voice was nearly as cold as his skin. "Who ordered the hit?"

"Cash is questioning the suspect now." Mason's gaze zeroed in on our clasped hands.

It was show of support and nothing more, but I could see it bothered Mason. I shifted forward, Aidan's hand slipping away, as I propped my elbows on my knees and rested my head in my hands.

This was the reason Mason reacted the way he did to my dream. Not because I hadn't told him right away – okay, that probably still had something to do with it.

"Damn Bean Nighe!" I jumped out of my seat and paced the small office. What I really wanted to do was get in on the interrogation and get a good look at my would-be assassin. I didn't bother to ask. I already knew Mason's answer.

"Is she speaking in tongues?" Amalie sounded concerned.

Aidan was equally confused. "I feel as if I have heard those words somewhere before. The meaning escapes me."

"It means I'm going to die."

You could have heard a pin drop. For a few seconds, no one spoke. I think they were shocked to hear those words come out of my mouth. I usually rushed in, asked no questions, took no prisoners. I risked my life every day as a Regulator. This was different. I liked to face problems head on.

Unfortunately, this time my problem could be coming from any direction.

"It means you *could* die. She doesn't control your fate, just warns you of it." Mason moved from behind his desk and stood in front of me. "Stop. Stop pacing and look at me. You're not allowed to die. I forbid it." He pulled me into a quick hug. "We'll figure this out together. Sit down. We're almost done and then I'll take you home."

"I don't want to go home. I want to see the person Cash is questioning. I've got a few questions of my own." I shifted back until I was able to see Mason's face. "Why is Cash running the interrogation anyway? I should be in there."

"Two reasons. One, the hitman is a were. According to the Meneur de Loupes agreement, when a rogue wolf comes into an Alpha's territory he is to be notified and given first right to question the rogue. Second, he's military trained. Some of Cash's methods may be frowned upon in civilized society, given the right subject they can be effective."

"You can't expect me to sit at home and wait to be taken out. To just do nothing."

"Until we know more, yes, that's exactly what I expect you to do." Giving me a sympathetic look, he shifted his gaze to the still, quiet woman laden down with pastries, "Amalie, send word to the Council about the bounty. Make sure Kellen knows about the Bean Nighe." He paused and cleared his throat before continuing. "Aidan can you take over for Maurin for awhile?"

Amalie was on her phone and running out of the office before Aidan could reply. "Of course I can. I'll contact our team and let them know before I go down for the day."

"Wait a minute, wait a goddamned minute." Was I freaked out there could be people lining up to kill me? Yes. Was I ready to cower in my apartment while they tried? Hell no. "Don't do this. Don't take my work, my team, away from me. I'll be careful. I promise, no unnecessary risks."

"How can you track if you're being tracked yourself?" Mason arched a brow, waiting for an answer.

Damn it, I hate it when he makes a point I can't argue against.

"I'll make the calls." Aidan wasn't going to be roped into one of our oldest arguments - my judgment where my safety was concerned. He obviously agreed with Mason.

"Wait! Mas, please." I wasn't above begging. "I won't do anything stupid. Don't lock me in my apartment like some princess in a tower."

He softened at the sound of desperation in my voice before turning to Aidan. "How hard would it be to make Maurin's apartment home base for the team? She could run the operations from there with the bonus of extra security."

"It might work." Aidan scratched his jaw. "If they make a move on the team or interfere with one of our cases, we'll need to reevaluate the plan."

"It's the best I can offer you right now, Maurin. What do you say, do we have a deal?"

"Having a tail would make my job difficult, not impossible." I held up a hand to silence the onslaught of arguments from both of them. "Still, I don't want to do anything which might put my team at risk which means no tracking. That does not mean I am not in charge. I still run the show. The team meets at my place before and after an assignment unless the sun is an issue."

"And you'll stay put, at least until we figure out who's trying to kill you." Mason left no room for further negotiations.

"Deal." I wasn't thrilled with the idea of being stuck in my apartment. It's harder to hit a moving target, but they were right. I was a liability out in the field right now. I didn't want someone getting hurt or killed because of me.

Mason and Aidan let out a collective breath as if they'd been expecting more of a fight. I'd been accused of being reckless with my own life. I tried not to be so cavalier when it wasn't just my ass on the line.

2

As promised, Mason attempted to escort me home after the meeting. We passed the interrogation room on our way out of the station. I begged him to let me sit in with Cash. Mason wasn't going for my idea of the good cop/bad cop routine. I tried to argue I had a right to question the person who had been sent to kill me. He argued I brought more emotion and tension to a situation where there was already too much of both.

I knew he was right. I felt helpless. Useless.

It sucked.

Mason opened the door to our right and nudged me inside. I could barely contain my excitement when I realized what he was doing.

"Thanks."

"The look on your face was thanks enough." He repositioned the massive file under his arm and pulled me into a half hug, kissing the top of my head. "Look, I know it's killing you to be kept off this case, especially when you're the target and one of the best interrogators in Salem. You have to trust me. I'll keep you updated. You'll have full access to files. Of course that means you have to promise you won't go after them."

"You think whoever hired this guy will send someone else?"

"When they realize you're still alive? Yeah, I do."

"Then I'm dead."

Mason jerked away from me, the color in his face draining. "I'm not going to let that happen."

Too late I realized how my previous statement could have been taken. "I meant, what if everyone thinks I'm dead?"

Mason stared at me for a long moment before shaking his head. "There's no way this guy would fall in line with that kind of plan. Once we cut him loose and we'll have to because all we have right now is suspicion, he's either going to try and take another shot at you or get the hell out of Salem. My money's on the latter. He knows we'll be watching him and he won't get another chance to seal the deal."

"Damn, for a second there I thought I had a plan. Is this my copy?" I tapped the file wedged between his elbow and ribs.

"A little bedtime reading. I meant what I said--just because I'm asking you to sit this one out doesn't mean I don't value your input."

With the flick of a switch, we could see into the room next to us. Cash sat on one side of the table - the same rectangular steel table I had questioned countless subjects at while working as a psychometric interrogator for SPTF - and the suspect sat on the other.

He was definitely a werewolf, a rogue with no fear of an alpha like Cash. Only, I doubt he'd ever come across an alpha like Cash before. He was arrogant for someone sporting a pair of Salem's finest silver cufflinks. The blisters were visible through the two-way mirror.

"His name is Jack 'TheRipper' London."

I rolled my eyes. "Let me guess, he's from England and he favors a blade."

"Wales, actually, and yes, if he can get close enough. Slitting the throat is his preference although he also enjoys a good disembowelment." He nodded at the file I clutched to my torso. "Still, according to his jacket, he's not opposed to shooting his target... He's been known to run with the Devil's Kin biker gang and has a rap sheet thicker than the Oxford dictionary."

"And he isn't serving life without parole because...?"

"The usual--a lot of circumstantial without enough physical evidence." Mason snorted and shook his head. "No body, missing witnesses, an alibi which is legally rock solid. Translation, total bull shit."

"Fantastic. So not only is he passionate about his work, he definitely has deep pockets behind him. How long has Cash been in there with him?" I couldn't recall the last time I'd used my psychometry to slip inside someone's mind, using the memory links in our fingerprints to gain access to the subconscious. My palms itched, sweat rolling down my back as I thought about all the condemning images I'd pulled out of perps' heads over the years. Something inside me woke up, a part of my gifts I hadn't used in a long time. I didn't miss my old job, or the life that went with it, just the use of that particular skill set.

Mason brought me back to the moment when he finally answered my question. "About half an hour longer than I expected. And we still haven't gotten anything. If he's half as smart as his file suggests, he's going to lawyer up here soon."

We continued to watch in silence as Cash drew on his pack magic to dominate the rogue wolf. Goosebumps covered my skin and the cloying scent of earth mixed with musk seeped into our little room through the vents. Any other wolf would cower under the weight of Cash's power, not London. He brushed the attempt at forced submission off like it was nothing.

Cash would be within his rights to assume London's refusal to submit was a challenge. Rogues didn't just stumble into a territory without contacting the alpha first. Unless they were looking for trouble.

"You can't withstand the weight of the pack much longer London. Who hired you?" Cash's voice crackled through the intercom.

"I ain't telling you, shit. That quim in there?" London jerked a thumb toward the mirror. "Yeah, she's in there. I can smell her. Why don't she bring that fine piece of arse in here and ask me herself?"

I looked at Mason, all but begging him with my eyes to let me go in there. My abilities had grown since I left SPTF. I knew I could find the information we needed if they'd just give me the chance. Mason chose to ignore my silent plea.

A low growl rattled the two way glass as Cash pulled harder on the pack magic to break London's will. Again London shook it off, flipping Cash the finger.

"I don't know how you're doing it, you're not an alpha. That's okay. I've got other ways of making you talk." Cash's hand partially shifted. Elongated fingers with razor sharp claws gripped the table. The metal groaned under the pressure.

"Mason." I touched his arm. "You need to pull Cash out of there."

"Give him a minute." He eyes remained locked on the two combative werewolves as he spoke. "Cash will pull it together. He's been trained for this."

"I've known Cash longer than you, trust me when I tell you we've moved beyond questioning and right into ripping out the jugular. He's about to go all big, bad, alpha wolf on that rogue and we'll end up with nothing." Widening my eyes, I jerked my chin at the smug bastard who'd thought he could kill me. "Right now, that's the only connection we have to whoever put out the contract on me. I don't feel like waiting for the next assassin to arrive to figure that out. Do you?"

"Son of a bitch." Mason rapped on the glass and stormed out of the room.

I stepped closer to the glass to get a better look at the guy. London's greasy hair was pulled back in a low ponytail sectioned off with rubberbands. His arms were covered in tattoos so old and faded they'd run together into one dark blue blob on his weathered skin. His leather jacket sporting the colors of the Devil's Kin was slung across the back of his chair. Worn black biker boots stuck out from under the table. London weighed in at two-seventy-five easy and had to be every bit of six-and-a-half feet. He'd spent a lifetime on the road with no alpha or pack to keep him in line and it showed in the way he carried himself. Hell, in the way he cared for himself, too, by the looks of his hygiene.

London turned as if sensing someone was watching him. He scented the air once. Twice. A wide, grey-toothed grin split his face. He drew his thumb across his throat as he mouthed the words, *"You're dead, bitch."*

Good thing Mason wasn't a betting man because I had a feeling he'd lose. London wasn't going to tuck tail and run. He had every intention of getting paid.

My hands burned with the need to touch him. Burrowed deep inside his thick skull was the name of the person who wanted me dead enough to pay someone to do the deed. A name I wanted so bad I could taste it. I heard Cash arguing with Mason in the hallway and briefly debated poking my head outside the door. A heated debate over whether or not

Cash should go back in was happening mere feet from me. If Cash couldn't go back in, the only qualified interrogator left in the building was me.

And then I remembered I wasn't an interrogator for SPTF anymore.

Fuck it. They needed me. Cash couldn't take away London's free will with his alpha mojo, forcing him to answer any questions. Masarelli couldn't find his way out of a paper bag, never mind find a way to get a killer like London to talk. I was the best and only chance we had before the wolf cried lawyer.

I moved to open the door, my hand hovering over the doorknob. The latch clicked, knob turned, signaling Mason's return,but I couldn't get out of the way fast enough. I took the brunt of the impact on my shoulder as Mason stormed back into the room.

"This is a total cluster fuck." He caught the door, saving me from another bruise as Cash barged in behind him.

"I can get him to talk, just not here." Cash clenched his hands, his claws fully retracted. All signs of the alpha outburst were gone.

"As tempting as that offer is, I can't let you take him." Mason was torn between his responsibility as captain of SPTF and as a member of the Wild Hunt. He knew better than most how this should play out. Unfortunately, London got picked up by two patrolman instead of one of the Council's people.

"I'm within my rights as alpha according to the Meneur de Loupes."

"He's trying to use the norms' legal system against us. He's here because of a bar fight. We don't have enough to charge him with anything more or to turn him over to you and he knows it." Mason turned toward the glass and crossed his arms. "If Mike doesn't press charges for damages to the bar or the guys he assaulted chicken out after they get bandaged up at the hospital, the most we can do is escort him to the city limits with a warning not to return without the proper paperwork." He clenched his jaw so tight his joints popped. "We need him to talk now."

I cleared my throat. My mouth went dry as the Sahara when they focused on me. The weight of their combined gaze almost had me second guessing myself. I swallowed hard and started to tell them my brilliant idea.

"No." Cash didn't let me get a single word out. "You're not going anywhere near him."

"I used to get paid to read guys like him. I'm offering my services pro bono to SPTF."

The room grew entirely too small as Cash and his wolf fought for control. "What part of 'he came here to kill you' are you not getting?"

"Pull back on the pack magic, would you? I live upstairs from you. You can't intimidate me." I started to roll my eyes, thought better of it, and smiled in what I hoped was a charming manner. "I'msimply asking to get a reading."

23

"Maurin, I've studied your case files." Mason stood his ground despite the look I gave him. "You've never had much luck with shifters."

"You read my case files?" My voice rose half an octave, ending on something close to a shriek.

Mason shrugged like it was no big deal. "I had Masarelli pull your files as soon as you walked out of my office after our first meeting. I needed to know what I was up against."

I knew he was talking about training me and possibly about his romantic pursuit of me. That didn't make me feel any better. I hugged the file closer to my chest, bothered by the idea he had a glimpse into my former life.

I used to categorize my life into Maurin Kincaide: unwanted family freak and Maurin Kincaide: SPTF's highly in demand hired freak. After I was possessed by a goddess to kill three other goddesses, my life could be compartmentalized into two different categories - before the Council and after the Council. I was proud of my work with SPTF, but I wasn't that person anymore.

I wasn't the outcast of a wealthy Boston family with psychic abilities, struggling to find her way in the world until the police came calling, only using her gifts when it was too late to save anyone. I wasn't on the side lines anymore, barely using an eighth of my potential. With the resurgence of my fae blood and my real father, Arawn, finally claiming me as his daughter, my powers and purpose were renewed. I hardly recognized that girl in those files and I hated the idea of him seeing me that way.

I stepped back as Mason reached for me and he froze, a puzzled look on his face. He'd picked up on my change of emotion, struggling to figure out what brought it on. Thankfully, before he had a chance to question anything, Cash spoke up, returning our focus to the pressing matter at hand.

"You're not touching him. You're not going in there, period. The pack will pick him up after his lawyer springs him."

I ignored Cash. The wolf was doing all of the thinking and I couldn't get anywhere with him when he was like that. Putting my hurt feelings aside, I turned to the person I could convince. "Mason, I'm your best chance and you know it. Stop treating me like a victim and see me as the asset I am."

"This is a terrible idea. I shouldn't be going along with this." Mason scrubbed his face. "Five minutes and you're not going in there alone."

Cash blocked the door. "Once you touch him, he'll have your scent. London will be able to track you. There's no hiding from a wolf like him."

My smile was more than a little grim. "I'm sure you and Nolak can come up with some creative ways to remind him what a terrible idea it would be to hunt me down on the ride to the city line."

Cash gave me a wolfish grin, his sharp canines peeking out. "After you."

I let out a breath, glad I had convinced the man and the wolf to go along with my plan. Mason was right about what my file said. In the three years I worked as an interrogator, I questioned at least a dozen shifters with minimal success.

The beast inside a shifter's mind is territorial. They chased me out before I could get too deep. The images I managed to pull were fuzzy at best. That was before a goddess took up residence inside my body like it was a Motel 6 when I had to take down the Morrigna. That was before I was claimed by my real father, Arawn, Lord of the Otherworld and my fae blood took over - before the Between marked me. I'd kicked literal demon ass and battled bat-shit crazy vampires. I could sort my way through one werewolf's mind.

3

I followed Mason and Cash into the interrogation room. They hung back by the door, giving me space to work. Power pulsed in my palm as I approached the table. London looked up. His gaze locked with mine in an optical game of chicken. He wanted to establish his dominance over me.

Fat chance of that ever happening.

"Hey pretty lady, suck cock?" London's laughter never reached his eyes. They held all the malice he had planned to unleash on me.

I smirked, my gaze unwavering, and dropped the file on the table. "Oh, baby, you say the sweetest things. How about we skip the pillow talk and go right to the part where you tell me what I want to know? Or we could do it the other way. You know, the one where I break into your mind and take what I want." My lips curved in a smile which held no humor. "It hurts. A lot."

He looked past me, trying to antagonize Mason and Cash. "You're making it too easy, bringing her in here."

Something flashed in his eyes, something that wasn't man or wolf. I didn't have time to process it. The silver cuffs groaned in protest as London forced his arms apart. The distinct smell of burning hair and flesh filled the room. Unable to withstand the pressure any longer, the metal gave out, freeing his hands. The chair he occupied seconds before crashed against the far wall as he lunged for me.

I braced my legs for the impact, my arms slightly outstretched as if to welcome him into an embrace. I knew with certainty once I had my hands on him, got inside his head, I could drop him. I sensed Mason and Cash moving in - one to grab me, the other to take London down.

Time slowed. Seconds felt like hours. I watched as London cleared the table. Waited for just the right moment to make my move.

One second too soon and I would come up with nothing but air. One second too late and he'd tackle me to the floor. The timing needed to be perfect.

I felt the warmth of his fetid breath on my face. We both clamped a hand on the other's throat. London would win in a battle of physical strength. Instantly, black spots danced along the edge of my vision. He brought his left hand around to apply more pressure and snap my neck. I caught it with my right, clasping our hands together.

I watched the look in his eyes switch from pleasure to panic and held on for dear life, rolling my body so I landed on top as we crashed to the floor.

With all my weight on his chest, I sat on top of a motionless London. I was inside his head. The wolf and the man cowered somewhere in his subconscious after my invasion. I couldn't see them, only feel them. He gave up control of his mind and body the moment I slipped inside.

Or did he?

I stood on a pile of rubble, the shattered remains of his mental blocks. Someone or something had been there before me - and they were sloppy. London had been nothing more than a host. Whatever had been residing inside his mind and body had fled, leaving a shell of a man behind.

Static noise filled the space inside his skull. I stepped off the debris and into the void left behind from the previous intruder. The energy shifted, became violent like an earthquake. Shit, he was seizing. I rushed to pull my power back, to get out of his mind before I did permanent damage.

Strong hands clamped down on my arms, yanking me off London's body. He jerked uncontrollably on the floor as I struggled to break the connection. The electrical impulses followed the mental tie like a conductor. I watched in horror as my fingers started to twitch.

"Let go of the link, Maurin, or you'll start convulsing. Let it go." Mason enveloped me, my body pinned against his, forearms crossed over my chest to control the small tremors racking my body.

Cash let out a low whistle. "London is broccoli."

"What?" Mason asked, still holding on to me.

"She cooked his brain. He's a fucking vegetable."

"Yeah? Well, *she's* about to be." Mason tucked my head beneath his chin, pinning it against his chest.

Cash rushed over to help, leaving a limp and lifeless London on the floor. The seizure ended for him almost as soon as it began. I prayed I would be as lucky.

"Don't touch her. Something isn't right."

"Understatement of the fucking year. She's having convulsions."

"It shouldn't be this bad--she didn't hold onto to the link that long. She actually listened for once and disconnected when I told her to."

For once? I might have been offended if I didn't resemble that remark.

In truth, I wasn't great at following directions. I made a silent promise to work on it.

As soon as the seismic activity racking my body stopped.

Despite being crushed in Mason's arms, I spasmed again. I tried to control my limbs, only they weren't responding. I couldn't stop shaking. In all the years I'd been using my psychometry to follow the links to people's memories, I'd never experienced anything like this. Hell, I didn't even know it was possible.

Mason did and for once he was wrong - I didn't let go in time. I held onto London too long, pulled out too late. Our minds linked, I experienced what he experienced. There was no other explanation for it.If we'd known he was epileptic, Mason probably wouldn't have let me go in.

It was a shame would-be assassins were so bad about wearing medical alert bracelets

Mason's hand was splayed across my abdomen, warmth radiating out from his touch. His energy filled my body, soothing the nerve endings and relaxing the constricted muscles and calming my mind before the seizure did too much damage. He moved through me, circulating through my veins like he was my life blood, until I was able to spindle enough energy of my own. The familiar sensation of the veil cascaded across my skin like cool water, cleansing a residue I hadn't realized was there.

The bitter taste of black magic clung to my mouth as I replaced the toxic spell with the Between. London's mind had been booby trapped. If I somehow managed to evade the assassination attempt and find my way inside his subconscious, "PlanB" would kick in—a mental time bomb set to detonate as soon as I followed the link.

Kill two birds with one stone. Erase London's mind and mine in one fell swoop.

Mason eased me into the only chair which remained upright. My ass barely connected with the seat before a well-dressed, smarmy individual who screamed *lawyer* walked in, escorted by Masarelli and two of SPTF's finest. He glanced at his would-be client, still on the floor, before zeroing in on me.

"I've been retained on Mr. London's behalf. Someone call for an ambulance. My client requires medical assistance." His voice was void of all emotion, his eyes were another story. Even in the panic that ensued when he requested an ambulance as Masarelli and the other officers raced to get the killer for hire medical attention, I saw the darkness in his eyes. A familiar malice flashed behind his dull brown eyes, the same malice I had seen in London's.

And all of it was focused on me.

I was certain I had never met this man before, but the fire of his hate scorched me from across the room. Too bad he didn't feel anything quite as passionate for his client. In fact, it seemed he couldn't care less.

It took ten minutes for Action Ambulance to arrive. Two paramedics ran in, pushing a gurney. One took vitals while the other asked questions about what happened. The next few minutes blurred by as they hurried to get London ready for transport. They worked with a speed and efficiency gained only after years of riding in an ambulance together. Throughout the entire process, the lawyer never took his eyes off me. Not even when they finally wheeled London out of the interrogation room.

"Captain, I will be escorting my client, who is catatonic thanks to that woman, to the hospital. Am I wrong to assume you have things in hand? I want a copy of her statement and the footage from the security tapes." The lawyer pointed to a small camera where the walls met the ceiling in the back right corner. He buttoned his dark gray blazer and straightened his black and white striped tie before walking out behind the last EMT.

Officers descended on cue. They separated the three of us, and proceeded to take our statements. I assumed Mason was escorted to his office. Cash was stuck at a desk out in the pit, while I was left alone in the interrogation room with my favorite detective- Masarelli. .

I tried to reign in my irritation. They were doing their job, following procedure with an inconvenient level of thoroughness I hadn't seen during my time with SPTF. The new captain had something to do with that. He demanded more of everyone around them, pushed them beyond the limits of what they thought they were capable of. I knew from experience, Mason did the same thing to me.

I didn't want the new and improved SPTF. I wanted shoddy police work and half-ass questioning which was something I'd come to expect from Masarelli. Mason and Cash didn't know about the black magic. I couldn't tell them while I was stuck answering all of Masarelli's damned questions. Questions that could have been answered by watching the security tapes. Which I knew he'd do repeatedly since my dress rode up.

We needed to know more about the spell hidden in London's mind. We needed to follow that attorney because I was convinced he was involved. I needed Masarelli to hurry the fuck up.

Masarelli had other plans.

"One more time.Explain to me why you were questioning the suspect instead of the Alpha." Masarelli made the word "you" sound dirty.

We were back to familiar territory. I'd finally convinced him we were telling the truth and hadn't done something to London to cause his seizure - which I kind of thought was obvious- and reached the point in the conversation where he liked to pretend he was a better interrogator than me.

"If you say one more time, *one more time*," I sighed. He was determined to ruin my day, more than it had been and that was saying something given my morning. I never thought I'd do this. Desperate times called for desperate measures. The trail went cold with every second that slowly, painfully ticked by. "You're right, they should have brought you in."

"What?" The disbelief was evident in his voice and on his face.

"You heard me." I prayed he heard me because I couldn't stomach saying it again.

"And why is that?" He was pushing his luck. Masarelli leaned forward when I didn't answer. "Why should they have brought me in when they had the all-powerful Maurin Kincaide with them?"

I wanted to punch him in his fat, smug face. Asshole, he wanted me say it. He finally had me backed into a corner. I hadn't done anything to London and everybody knew it. Still, the situation was suspicious. Moments after I touched him, he began convulsing. The tapes showed me suffering from the same affliction as London. Nothing that irrevocably proved I wasn't the cause, giving Masarelli the opportunity to drag out the questioning. The whole department knew Mason and I were dating. It looked bad enough that he let his girlfriend, who was no longer part of the team, into the room with London. It would probably raise a couple of eyebrows in internal affairs if he came to rescue me from Masarelli and his best interrogation technique- redundancy.

I could have asked for the human lie detector kept on SPTF's payroll, Pollyanna, but Masarelli would never have gone for it. Not after she cleared me on murder charges when I had to put the last alpha's wife down. If I wanted to do anything about the ticking time bomb London's attorney was walking around with inside his head, I had to tell Masarelli what he wanted to hear.

It was just one little sentence. My throat constricted. Five words I vowed never to speak, no matter how much he improved, no matter how many cases he managed to solve. Not even if by some miracle it became truth. I promised myself I wouldn't, under any circumstances, say those words to him. I felt nauseous.

"You're better than I am."

He jumped out of his chair. "That will be included in your official statement."

"I don't care if you take out a fucking billboard. We done here?" I wasn't sure if I could get up. I held my stomach, hoping the latte and croissant would stay inside. Who knew one stupid sentence could take so much out of you physically.

"We're done."

4

I walked past Mason's office, past the pit where Cash sat in a chair at the desk of a detective I didn't recognize. With fierce determination not to gag on the pride I'd choked down back in that room with Masarelli, I walked out of the station. I took a deep breath, closed my eyes and faced the sky to soak in the rejuvenating warmth of the sun as the morning's events replayed in my head.

Someone wanted me dead. While I wasn't completely shocked by the news, I still couldn't think of anyone who would go to the lengths of possessing a werewolf to do it. Or a lawyer for that matter. I didn't know what his role he played. I was certain of two things. One, it was more than just representing London. Two, I hadn't seen the last of him.

"You okay?"

I didn't answer right away. I felt like I sold my soul telling Masarelli he was better than me. I had a black magic-induced seizure and was indirectly responsible for turning London into a vegetable. Granted he was here to kill me, but I couldn't shake the feeling something else was going on. Not to mention the migraine from coffee deprivation.

"Never better." I turned around to face Cash, hiding the lie with a smile.

"You're full of shit. What the hell did you say to Masarelli? He looked like he was about to do back flips through the station."

"I said he was a better interrogator than me." The look of horror on his face had me scrambling to explain. "He was going to keep me in that damn room all day. Did you know SPTF can hold an Other for forty-eight hours without cause? I didn't have much choice."

"Ouch. No more get out of jail free cards now." Cash sidled up to me and swung an arm around my shoulders.

"Well let's hope I'm not in the room when somebody else dies in the station."

"Yeah, about that. What happened? One second you have your hands on him and the next you're both shaking like someone hooked you up to jumper cables. He was fried, I couldn't even sense his wolf after that. What did you do?"

"I didn't do anything." I tried not to sound defensive. "Did you see Mason? Is he coming? Because we need to get to the hospital, like now. I want to talk to that lawyer."

"You really think that's a good idea? He seemed pretty hell bent on pinning this whole thing on you. You might want to hold off on giving him any ammunition."

"I'll explain on the way. Let's just get Mason and go over there."

Before either of us had a chance to head back inside, Mason stormed out of the station. "We're going to the hospital. I'm driving."

Cash gave me a weird look. "I thought that was your line. What gives, you two can read each other's minds or something?"

"No." Then it dawned on me. We could communicate if at least one of us was in the Between. "Actually, yes." I shot Mason an accusatory glare- having the ability to call for help was one thing, eavesdropping was something entirely different.

"I wasn't listening to your conversation, Maurin. I'll explain on the way. Let's go." Mason headed for his truck.

"Seriously, stop stealing my lines." I shouted after him.

Cash and I raced to catch up with him. Well I raced, Cash didn't have to. Super speed wasn't one of my super powers. I had to double time it just to keep up with their regular, long-legged stride. I hoisted myself into the cab, pulling on the "oh shit" handle just above the door. I felt a hand on my ass, giving a little push. After sliding across the bench seat, I glowered at Cash.

"What? You looked like you needed a little help." He smiled devilishly as he fastened his seatbelt.

"If you're done groping my girlfriend, maybe we could go see about the dead attorney?"

Mason's black and white sixty-nine Chevy truck roared to life. He pealed out of the parking lot before either of us could ask him what happened. His ability to weave through traffic at high speeds and talk at the same time was impressive.

"We received a call from the ER. Apparently, one Mark Anderson, Esquire suffered a massive aneurysm in the waiting room while his client was being treated. He was dead before anyone realized what happened."

"And London?" I braced myself for his answer. I had a bad feeling our prime suspect saw his last sunrise.

"He's currently hooked up to life support. No sign of brain activity."

"Shit." Anger and frustration coursed through me. Whatever held London in its grip controlled the lawyer as well. We needed more information. Unfortunately neither of them were talking.

"So we have a dead lawyer and a brain dead werewolf." Cash looked out the window, watching the city blur by as he puzzled over what was going on. "We could force his change."

"You can't be serious." I gaped at him, then turned to look at Mason surprised to see he was considering it. "You want to make him shift, in a hospital? Full of Norms, while he's hooked up to all kinds of equipment?"

"He's not the first werewolf they've seen, Maurin." Cash shook his head, like I wasn't getting it.

"Right, because so many shifters end up in the hospital, it wouldn't freak the nurses out to have a man in the bed one moment and an enormous wolf in it the next."

"They've got staff specifically trained to deal with the shifter anatomy. There are occasions when even a werewolf is injured seriously enough to require outside help."

Another worry plagued my mind. Was there trouble in the pack? Had Cash been challenged, hurt badly enough defending his position that he had to seek help outside the pack? I'd seen Cash fight on more than one occasion. Hell, I was the witness to his challenge for Alpha of the Salem pack. The idea of someone sending him to the hospital seemed ludicrous. Still, he hadn't been Alpha long and I knew there were wolves loyal to the former alpha inside Cash's pack.

"You know this from experience? Is there trouble in the pack?"

He looked down at my hand-the one that had managed to find its way into his without my knowledge. "Nothing that I can't handle."

He didn't want to worry me, not with a bounty looming over my head. I pressed for more. "You were challenged?" He hadn't been around lately. I'd assumed he was busy with the pack. He'd been busy alright.

"Oh ye of little faith." He gave my hand a gentle squeeze. He held on a moment, reveling in the contact, the way his large hand engulfed mine. A sad smile tugged the corner of his mouth as he released his hold and set my hand back in my lap. "Nolak was challenged for his position as second. Something I don't think will happen again. He's happy for now. It won't be long before he leaves, that wolf is a born alpha."

"He wouldn't challenge you?" I hadn't meant for it to sound like a question. Nolak followed Cash to Salem. They were brothers in everything except blood.

"No." He didn't sound convinced.

"We're here." Mason pulled into a spot near the emergency entrance reserved for police vehicles.

Cash hopped out of the truck's cab, cut through the ambulance entrance and headed for the large, sliding doors marked for emergency personal only.

I made the leap from front seat to hard concrete before Mason could help me down, ignoring the sharp twang in the small bones of my right foot when it took the brunt of the impact. I grabbed his hand and started after Cash. Mason stopped short, my arm jerking a little. I snapped back to him like a rubber band.

He looked at my hand, wrapped up in his the same way Cash had, before looking at me. "What is he to you?"

"What?" The question came out of left field.

"Cash, what is he to you?" He searched my face for an answer.

"I heard the question. I'm just not sure what you're asking."

"I see the way he looks at you. Part of the reason I'm letting him help on this investigation is because I know he'd do anything to find out who's trying to hurt you."

"We're just friends." I tried to reassure him.

"You sure about that?" Mason tilted his head slightly and looked at Cash, who waited for us outside the entrance.

"He knows where I stand." I laced my fingers through his and tightened my grip on his hand.

Mason lifted our entwined hands, turning them until my fingertips rested against his lips. His eyes closed for a moment. His warm breath caressed my skin as he exhaled. He was reading me, not the way I did, not my memories, just my emotions. I'd never let someone do that without my permission before. It was different with Mason. Everything was different with Mason. I wanted him to know how I felt.

"You coming or what?" Cash called out before stepping into range of the door sensor. The glass doors slid open and he walked through.

Mason and I followed, hands still locked together, determined to find something, anything pointing us in the direction of the person orchestrating my demise.

Cash was already questioning the triage nurse when we came in. He leaned against the entrance to her small room filled with equipment, a laptop on one of those portable stands and a chair for the patient. He hit her with his bad boy charm, one that no doubt left a string of broken hearts in his wake. She was a wink and a crooked grin away from needing to be hooked up to the blood pressure and pulse ox monitors herself.

It never ceased to amaze me how different he was from the first time I met him. My loyalties were firmly planted with the former alpha and his wife at the time. I couldn't believe it when Cash actually challenged him for the pack. My allegiance shifted when a witch killing demon was unleashed in town last year. Somewhere between discovering the Coven's betrayal and killing the demon, Cash and I became friends.

He'd saved my ass on more than one occasion and I would gladly do the same for him.

I watched him work his magic with the nurse and suddenly understood Mason's need for reassurance. Aidan and I had an instant attraction. It was a torrent of emotions from beginning to end, destined to burn out quickly from the heat between us.

Cash, on the other hand, was a sleeper agent. Our relationship was rooted in friendship, easily developing into something more if both people wanted it to. One of us did, or thought they did. That would change when he met his true mate.

I wondered if our friendship would survive the woman who tamed him. I couldn't imagine my life without him in it. He called me out on my bullshit and kept me in check. The only other person to do that was Mason. Trust me when I tell you it's a full time job and Mason could use the help.

The nurse pulled London and Anderson's charts up on her laptop. Apart from a bunch of medical jargon, there wasn't anything new to learn. The medical examiner was on the way over to pick up Anderson's body. I had more confidence in a report that came out of the ME's office than anything we'd learn here.

Jacobs was trained in more than the human anatomy. As a mystic, she had the unique ability to sense magical causes of death. Needless to say, natural causes graced fewer death certificates after Jacobs took the job here in Salem. We'd have to wait until she completed her examination of Anderson's body before we knew what caused the aneurysm.

I leaned against the doorjamb, watching the bustling activity in the emergency room and waited for the guys to reach the same conclusion I had - this was a dead end. We were just spinning our wheels until the ME report came in.

Alarms dinged from monitors inside the nurse's station. Scrubs in varying colors flashed by as nurses and interns rushed to a room down the hall, the rubber on the soles of their sneakers squeaking on the tile floor. Another doctor whizzed past pushing a paddle cart.

Mason and Cash ignored the commotion common in any hospital and continued to read through the charts. Dread settled in my stomach as an orderly charged down the hall. I knew the activity came from London's room.

I elbowed Mason, momentarily drawing his attention from the monitor. "Something's going on."

"It's a hospital Maurin, something is always going on." His eyes widened as red alert bars flashed across the screen, highlighting London's name. "Let's go. Room six."

"Shouldn't be hard to find." I followed him to London's room.

Cash said goodbye to the nurse, giving her a wink when she slipped him her number and made him promise to call.

The three of us ran side by side past the first two rooms until a nurse pushing a kid in a wheelchair forced us to go single file. Mason led the way, the smell of antiseptic and illness getting stronger the further down the hall we went. Hospitals freaked me out. My ability to heal came with a beefed up immune system. I wouldn't catch anything during our visit, but my skin itched and my hands involuntarily shot out under the automatic sanitizer dispenser when we reached room six.

A long, steady beep greeted us at the door. The telltale sound that someone's heart stopped. A doctor confirmed it when he called the time of death. The rush of people moving and the quiet hum of the paddles charging died the second London did.

The cold snap of latex gloves being removed broke the somber moment. One after the other, doctors and nurses shuffled out, heads down. The group dispersed, off to treat other patients and hopefully save lives. They didn't know London came to Salem with the sole purpose of killing me. I wondered if their heads would still be hung with disappointment and the shame of failure if they did.

"Dead men tell no tales. I guess we're back to square one, which is located on the corner of clueless and no fucking idea." Cash let out a frustrated sigh, raking fingers through his cropped black hair.

"Maybe they do." London yielded no results before his brain was fried. Any residual memories on his belongings were already gone. The lawyer's property on the other hand, I could work with. "Let's go see Jacobs."

"If she's started the autopsy, it will be too late." Mason pulled out his phone and started dialing as he took off for his truck with Cash and me on his heels. "Jacobs, it's Hunter. Don't crack the skull."

5

The morgue was right up there with hospitals on my list of most undesirable places. Unfortunately, Anderson couldn't come to me. I had to go to him. The last time I was here to read the deceased I needed a little help. It was easy to become lost in the pain typically found in someone's last memory. I tried it once on my own - at the insistence of Mahalia. It was a disaster. So the next time we found ourselves with more bodies than clues, Aidan arranged for some back up. Graive funneled her necromancy through the body of a murdered young woman into me. My power in turn was pushed back through the victim into Graive. The circulation of our abilities was the only reason I could see the memories at all.

I had no intention of touching Anderson's dead body. Personal effects worked just fine - enough for a few memory flashes anyway. I got a hit off a laptop once, led us right to a demon. All I needed was a fingerprint. And a fresh body. Oh, and his brain intact. If Jacobs sawed open his skull and poked around inside his head, it wouldn't work. Nothing worked once the brain was exposed.

Jacobs waited for us in the hallway, pissed off we delayed her examination. Apparently she had a life. At least one of us did. I felt the walls of my apartment pressing in on me and I hadn't been home yet. Mason probably had a house arrest ankle bracelet hidden in his glove compartment.

She slapped a small, clear, plastic bag in my hand and raised a quizzical brow at my disappointed expression. "You were expecting more? The guy was dead at least twenty minutes before someone noticed. Be thankful you got a wedding band, his wallet and a pen. I'm willing to bet he had a pretty decent watch on when he went into the ER. Someone in the waiting room probably slipped it off while he was sleeping." She made air quotes around the word sleeping.

"The guy was a high-priced defense lawyer. I'd say the watch was better than decent. Probably turn up at a pawn shop in a day or two. It'll be useless by the time we find it, too many overlapping prints." I looked at the contents of the bag again.

The wallet would have given me the strongest connection if Anderson hadn't kept his wallet in his back pocket.The fabric would have smudged any decent prints when he sat down.

"Unless it was a Rolex, I would have taken the pen." Jacobs tapped the baggie and let out a low whistle. "Damn thing costs more than I make in a month."

While that was obviously an exaggeration, it was an expensive pen. One Mr. Anderson likely used often - he probably pulled the pen out more than the wallet. Jacobs eyeballed me from across the hall, her patience wearing thin. I pointed toward her office and excused myself from the conversation. She let out a sigh, reminding me again she had things to do and that I needed to hurry.

Mason followed me into the cramped office, leaving very little room to work. I didn't need much space; he simply sucked the oxygen out of the room. Or maybe it was just me, I seemed to have trouble breathing around him.

Careful not to contaminate the rest of the contents, I removed the pen from the bag. Images flooded my mind immediately, too fast and fuzzy to be of any use. I forced my mind to slow down and focus on one picture at a time. I watched Anderson slipping the pen into his inside jacket pocket before heading to work, signing legal document after legal document before finally taking a call about London's arrest. His last day unfolded, yielding nothing useful. The link faded faster than I hoped and I had nothing that led us to the person who wanted me dead.

I came to the last hour of his life. Anderson walked into the interrogation room full of confidence and a hint of superiority. I saw myself through his eyes and tried not to be offended when I felt his immediate dislike. The spell jumped from London to Anderson a split second later. His heart unknowingly pumped the black magic through his body and mind. It hit him hard and fast.

Hate coiled inside his body like a viper waiting to strike, while the darkness over took his soul. There was nothing left of the man. Norms couldn't withstand a spell of this potency. He didn't have a snowball's chance in hell of surviving.

I felt the magical remnants seep through the link like an oil spill, contaminating everything around it. Something in the spell recognized me, felt me moving inside Anderson's memories. Black tendrils whipped out through the memory links. The caster of this spell was powerful, really powerful.

I dropped the pen before it was too late. As much as I wanted to know who created that spell, I wasn't suicidal. Enough black magic remained inside Anderson to do some real damage. Hanging on for a few seconds longer, trying to get a glimpse of the source, would only get me killed. The spell was parasitic, jumping from host to host. I wasn't any closer to figuring out who wanted to kill me or stopping them. And that last part was important because I'm pretty keen on the whole living thing.

Mason wrapped his arms around my waist and pulled me into him, resting his chin on the top of my head. "What did you see?"

"It's a parasite. It can move from body to body. How do we stop something like that? That makes everyone a suspect. I can't stay locked up in my apartment forever." I turned my head up to look at him. The intensity of his gaze mixed with his dazzling good looks took my breath away. Maybe house arrest wouldn't be so bad after all.

I felt his body shake with silent laughter. "I said that last part out loud, didn't I?"

"Yes." Mason's smile had my stomach doing summersaults. "For all your complaining about being trapped in your apartment, you do realize you haven't spent one minute there since this whole mess started?"

I wanted to protest. It didn't matter if I hadn't been home yet because as soon as I got there, I wouldn't be leaving. His hand trailed along my side and my mind went blank.

"You won't be able to send me home, Maurin. I'm heading up your security detail and I'm taking the night shift."

My heart skipped a beat. The thought of waking up with him, both of us still sleepy eyed and suffering from bed head thrilled and terrified me. Mason was the kind of man who would ruin you for all others. I wanted him; needed him so badly and it scared the ever loving shit out of me. Over the solstice holiday I realized Mason was it for me. That moment of clarity was immediately followed by the irrational fear that any moment he'd realize he could do better.

"Is the prospect of waking up next to me every morning really so terrifying?" He cupped my face, tilting my head back until our eyes met. "Will you run screaming from the room if I tell you I love you?"

"Mason, I... I.''The words were there on the tip of my tongue. No matter how many times I tried, they wouldn't come out. I thought I was in love a couple of times, all of that paled in comparison to Mason. He reduced me to a stammering school girl with one question. One question I desperately wanted to answer, if the words weren't stuck in my throat. "I..."

Mason's mouth found mine, stopping my stutter with a passionate kiss. He pulled back, still holding my face in his massive hands. He must have seen what he was looking for in my eyes. "I know, Maurin. I know." He wrapped me back up in his powerful arms, resting my head against his chest. "Tell me more about the spell. You felt it in London?"

Back on solid ground and relieved for the change in topic, my heart rate slowed and my ability to speak coherently returned. "Yeah, I wanted to tell you, but with the detainment and people dying we haven't had time."

"It's certainly been a busy morning." His fingers kneaded my lower back, working out some of the tension.

"London was different though. He wasn't in control. He was still in there, so was his wolf. Something took over his mind."

"I knew something was wrong, I just couldn't figure out what."

"So, you couldn't sense the magic?"

"Not like you, no. You backed out of London's mind in time, you shouldn't have been effected. I didn't feel anything before then."

"If I stayed in his head a couple more minutes, I would have been in a hospital bed next to him. It was like a psychic bomb or something."

"So the spell that fried London's brain wasn't the same as the one to control him?"

"Mas, you're a genius. Come on, I want to ask Jacobs something." I opened the office door, dragging Mason behind me and rushed into the exam room.

Jacobs finished the Y incision and was preparing to crack Anderson's ribs. "You finished already?" The question dripped with sarcasm. "No need to rush on my account. I already canceled my lunch date."

I ignored her feeble attempt at whining. She quit being mad the second she started the examination. "How powerful would you have to be to layer spells inside someone's mind?"

"What do you mean by 'layer'? Like you went in and spelled someone after they'd already been spelled?"

"No, like you cast one spell for one thing and then another spell for something else?"

"An intermediary witch could accomplish layered spells. It's not as difficult as you think. It can get messy so you don't see it very often. If you're through," She waved a hand toward Anderson's body. "I'd like to get back to work. You'll have my report as soon as I'm done."

Disappointment must have shown on my face because she promised to call if she discovered anything unusual with the body or the spells. I'd hoped to leave the morgue with more than the possibility of a phone call. It seemed like nothing was going my way.

We had more questions than answers on the ride back to my apartment. Cash wanted to dig deeper into London and Anderson's backgrounds. A few ex-military guys specializing in intel owed him a favor and Cash planned to meet them at Brewed Awakening. Until we narrowed down our list of suspects - which was just about everyone at this point - a normal hangout was the safest place. He went back decades with these guys, but wasn't taking any chances. We dropped him off at the coffee shop half an hour before his friends were due to meet him, giving him plenty of time to scope the place out.

Mason planned on following the magic after I convinced him the spell could have been transmitted to someone else before Anderson died. He took me home before heading back to the hospital for a list of staff members who handled the lawyer's body and any patients waiting to be seen while he was there. HIPA laws required a warrant; Mason was willing to push the envelope on this one.

Meanwhile, I sat in my apartment and poured over the file Mason gave me. It didn't take long to read and even less time to research. Even my beloved Google let me down. There was nothing on the net I hadn't learned in London's rap sheet.

The only new information I came across were Captain Matthison's notes scribbled on the margins of my reviews. While his assessments of my skills and psychological state were insightful, they didn't get me any closer to finding our man. Or woman.

I needed a break from London and the plot to kill me.

Another file on my table required my attention. Agrona emailed an assignment from the council; I'd printed it out while researching the Bean Nighe with the intent to review the profile and map out the run. Mason called and I never got the chance. It was a welcomed distraction.

A small coven of dark witches cropped up outside of Danvers. Without a high priestess to oversee the magical community in Salem and the surrounding areas, blood magic began to take root and the Council finally took notice.

The council stunted the coven as part of the punishment for their role in Mahalia's betrayal. Permanently stripped of the council seat, they lost their voice within the governing body. Without the ability to elect their own leader without council approval, they lost control of the coven. The council unknowingly created the perfect breeding grounds for black magic.

Next in line to lead the coven, Oberon unofficially became the high priest. The majority of witches quietly followed his lead, regardless of the council's decree. There were a few who couldn't resist the temptation. Blood magic came quicker and easier than earth magic. It also came with a higher price - your soul.

Human familiars cropped up on the outskirts of town. Witches who used people to store magical energy were shunned and eventually eliminated. Without a universally recognized figurehead,the shunning stopped. Left unchecked, this posed a real danger to the norms and was a direct violation of the post shift cohabitation agreements.

A carefully worded recommendation to acknowledge Oberon as high priest had been in my last report. The Council ignored it. My team snuffed out the dark witches whenever they popped up. It was a losing battle when another would just take their place. We couldn't stop them all.

Frustrated and discouraged, I finished preparing the plan for our latest attempt and emailed an update to the council.

6

Bored and stir crazy.

Those were the two best words to describe me. I checked the time, almost eleven. Three hours after I finished my reports and I was ready to climb the walls. I wasn't the only one. Conry dropped his leash at my feet. House arrest threw a serious wrench in our routine. Twice a week we ran a few miles around town.The other days we slipped into the Between so he could recharge and really stretch his legs. He'd been stuck in the apartment longer than me and wanted to run...

"Sorry buddy. We're going to have to wait a while longer," I said, scratching behind his ears. He left the leash where it lay and headed off to our bed. I used to think I shared my bed with him. I was wrong. I lost more and more of the mattress to my dog every day.

With Nolak out on a perimeter check, and another wolf posted at the entrance to my building, I was locked up tight. I was as safe as could be and going completely out of my mind. I should have been out chasing leads with Mason or Cash, not sitting around my apartment - a part of the solution, not just part of the problem.

I vacuumed, dusted, cleaned the bathroom and even the fridge. I scrubbed the kitchen floor while I waited for the cycle on the dryer to finish. I alphabetized my pantry and my bookshelves, organized my underwear drawer and color coordinated my closet- which didn't take long since the majority of my clothes are black. I even sorted my band tee shirts by music genre and name. My place had never been so clean - not even on the day I moved in.

I ate an entire pint of Ben and Jerry's "That's My Jam" for lunch, which left me with an unusual combination of brain freeze and sugar high. Daytime TV sucked. Four-hundred channels on my premium cable subscription and not a single thing to watch. After scrolling through the program guide three times, still scraping the bottom of the ice cream carton, I was convinced my ass had already begun to spread.

When I'd removed the lid and dug in -with a tablespoon no less- I'd convinced myself that the vitamin D and calcium in the ice cream, antioxidants in the chocolate, plus the raspberry fruit swirl classified it as a health food. One episode of The Dr. Oz Show changed my mind.

Riddled with guilt over my dairy indulgence, I pushed the coffee table against the wall and the love seat in front of it. With my living room shoved into one corner, I had a fairly decent-sized space to work out.

The Metallica playlist I created on Pandora blared from the Bose speakers connected to my Galaxy S4. All Nightmare Long came on as I picked my daggers up off the floor. I practiced regularly with my sword. My skill with daggers needed some improvement.

With my height disadvantage, I took a lot of damage working my way inside with a short blade. Speed coupled with an onslaught of hits was the only way I could get in close. If I planned on being faster than a vampire, or even a werewolf, I had to practice.A lot. And it wasn't like I didn't have the time.

Sweat dripped off my body and soaked into my clothes. Half an hour into my work out, I added silver stakes. An hour after that, all the muscles in my body burned so I switched to the Deftones for my cool down routine. Swerve City came on as I chugged a bottle of ice cold water. I grabbed a towel out of the linen closet, preparing for a shower, just as someone knocked on the door.

It had to be one of the guys on guard duty. I checked the peep hole anyway. Safety first, right? The guy who lived on the first floor - forever called "hey man", since I couldn't remember his name and gave up trying a couple months ago - stood in the hall.

Relatively confident he wasn't here to kill me, I opened the door.

"Hey man, what's up?" I leaned on the doorjamb hoping to avoid any sentences that would require his name.

He gave me an irritated look. I couldn't blame him, I tended to have that effect on people. Hey man just stood there, silently staring me down.

My neighbor stood out in my hall, pissed off for reasons only he knew. He gave off a weird vibe and still hadn't said anything.

"So what can I do for you? Is the music too loud or something?" I kept it light, tried to get him to say something.

Again with the silent treatment.

He blinked hard and I noticed his eyes for the first time. The pale blue color of his eye was dulled by a milky white film. Maybe he was sick, with an eye infection and laryngitis. Or maybe, I needed to shut the fucking door. I gave a short whistle for Conry. He didn't respond. Not so much as a growl.

I slammed the door and rushed to grab my cell, calling out for my guardian again. The front door crashed against the wall as I hit send call. In my haste, I forgot to lock it. Hey man barreled in past the wards etched into the framing, his movements stiff and jerky.

Mason warded my apartment against anything or anyone that meant me harm. The animated corpse staggering closer shouldn't have been able to get inside. I expected Conry to burst from the bedroom. He never came. I called his name again. *Where was he?* As much as I worried for my guardian, the newly dead had to be my first priority because he looked hungry and was closing the distance between us.

The dead man walking was freshly made. The telltale stench of rot was barely noticeable under his cologne. Frozen vocal chords and filmy eyes were the only notable symptoms.

Whoever turned him into a zombie left no physical trace of how they killed him.

My bodyguards weren't the only ones keeping an eye on me.Its maker knew I was locked down, knew who would be allowed access in and out of the building. They knew I was home and who I kept close.

My daggers were on the floor a couple of feet in front of the walking worm food. Tossing my phone, I dropped and rolled, scooping up my knives. I shoved one into his knee, severing the meniscus. His leg crumpled under the weight of his body, sending me scurrying back on all fours to get out of the way as he collapsed.

Graive Larrick was the only necro in Salem. She wasn't my biggest fan, but I couldn't see her turning my neighbor into a zombie. She was sleeping with Oberon. She had an entire coven at her disposal. Magic that wouldn't lead right back to her. If she wanted me dead she had other means. And she definitely wasn't strong enough to take Conry out on her own. *Was someone else raising zombies in Salem?*

"Conry!" I yelled again. He never abandoned his post, never.

I was his anchor to Salem. The tether that connected his energy to mine had been severed. I no longer felt the pull on my chi which allowed us to be separated for any length of time. Without an active link between us, he should have returned to the Hunt – which would have alerted my father.

Arawn wasn't here which meant Conry wasn't with him. The zombie was a fucking decoy.

My dead neighbor dragged himself across the floor faster than I expected with only two functional limbs. He grabbed my ankle, pulling me to him. Caught off guard by his strength, I went down. My back burned as the berber carpet rubbed against it. I kicked at his face with my free foot, snapping his head back. He didn't let go. The second dagger went deep into his forearm as he clamped his jaws around my calf. He tore off a chunk of muscle, greedily gulping it down as I screamed before he started biting down again - this time into my thigh.

Something cool and rough like wet sandpaper ran along my thigh. Bile burned the back of my throat when I realized it was a cold dead tongue lapping up the blood steadily dripping from the wound. I pulled the dagger free of his arm and jammed it into his temple. He gnawed at my flesh as I turned the blade, forcing it deeper into his skull. That worked in the movies. Reality proved once again to be a cold, heartless bitch when the corpse's teeth moved further into my flesh, to tearing off another piece of me.

Nolak ran in with his gun raised, knocking the broken door out of the way. I shouted for him to stop, not to shoot. He couldn't hit the zombie without hitting me. I had no idea what type of ammo Nolak had in his gun or how it would affect me. He fired one shot. The bullet ripped through the zombie's head, out his jaw and into my thigh. I screamed again. The remnants of my neighbor's head covered me and my walls.

I'd never see a penny of my security deposit.

"Cash said this was a good building, nice neighbors. Is there somebody else besides you and the corpse living here?" Nolak held out a hand to help me up.

"The demon attack was hardly my fault."

Nolak's brows went up to his hairline, guess he hadn't heard that story. About a year ago,the Inquisitors -a group of religious extremists- came to take out the coven. They unleashed one of the demons captured by Solomon and forced to build his temple -an Afrit. They believed the beast had been converted by the king. It wasn't. I tried to kill him, and then he ate the old lady who used to live in Cash's apartment and tried to kill me.

I pointed to the body that quickly began to rot after its head exploded. "And that's not my fault either."

Nolak shrugged unconvinced.

"You're right. Cash should probably move." I wiped a chunk of zombie brain off my face and slung it on the floor.

Nolak's eyes followed the chunk of meat, cringing when it hit the floor with a squishing sound. "We might all be safer if you moved. To the country, in one of those old farm houses in the middle of nowhere. Miles from civilization."

"Funny." I ground out as a painful burn made its way up from the wound in my calf to my thigh. I stumbled across the room to the love seat shoved in the corner so I could get a better look at it.

I rolled my pant leg up and examined the bite. Familiar red lines spider webbed out from it. Who knew what kind of toxins were in the corpse's mouth? The Afrit caused a similar reaction when he ripped me apart with his claws.

Aidan saved my ass, drawing the Afrit's poison out with a bite, unfortunately that option wasn't available anymore. My blood was addictive to vampires - one of the many reasons our relationship had to end. Giving him more, even to cleanse my blood was a bad idea.

"Call Mason." I peeled back the veil, enough for some of the energy to seep into me, careful not to slip inside. I promised Mason I wouldn't go anywhere alone, even into the Between.

Questions filled my mind as the effects of shock and blood loss spread through my body. *Who had my dog, who made the zombie, who were they working for and what the hell did it all have to do with me?*

My teeth chattered.The chills pulled me away from puzzles I didn't have all the pieces to solve and back to my injuries. I spindled more of the Between, drawing it into my chi, wishing I could slip inside to take advantage of the increased healing speed. Mason was on his way, he'd fix whatever I couldn't heal on my own.

Nolak lifted me up off the floor and helped me to the bathroom. "Take off your pants and sit on the counter."

Circumstances what they were, his demands were neither forward nor provocative. Nothing about my body was sexual, flesh was flesh. Wounds needed to be assessed and treated. The cotton bikini briefs I wore provided little barrier against the cold porcelain sink, but they might as well have been armor plated where Nolak was concerned- which was totally fine with me.

"What are you looking for?" I pulled the stopper on the sink, filling the basin with warm water.

"Disinfectant." He closed the mirrored door of my medicine cabinet, before moving to the cabinet under the sink.

"I don't have any. I think I can heal this if you just help me clean up the blood." I dropped a wash cloth in the water, watching it float on the surface like a jellyfish before settling against the bottom.

"Mason can't get through the Between. He's on his way. It'll take him about twenty minutes to get here. He said to disinfect the bite before wrapping it." Nolak slid bottles of shampoo and Lord knew what else, around in the cabinet.

"I'm pretty sure my first aid kit is empty. I haven't really had a need for one lately."

"Is that so?" He shook his head, chuckling.

"You're hilarious, really. Wait a sec, what do you mean Mason can't get through the Between? He can't jump here?"

"I don't even know what that means. I think I found something." He held up an old bottle, the label worn and barely legible.

"I'm pretty sure that came with the apartment. Whatever it is, it's expired." He unscrewed the cap. "Seriously, you're not putting that on me."

Searing pain flared as he poured the brownish liquid over the first bite wound. "Holy shit, that burns. Wait, wait don't put it on the other one!" I cursed, called him a few names and punched the counter. "What the fuck is that stuff?"

"Mercurochrome."

"Are you serious? They don't even sell that stuff anymore. God, that burns."

"Got any gauze?" Nolak managed to ask through the laughter.

"I didn't have any peroxide, what makes you think I'd have gauze?" The urge to kick him square in the balls was strong, somehow I resisted.

"I'll have to find something to make a bandage. Once we get you patched up, you need to take it easy, lie down and let your body take over the healing process. Sit tight, I'm going to grab a shirt, cotton is probably the best bet."

I jumped down off the counter, my legs wobbling. "Oh no, no way.You're not going through my closet unsupervised. You'll probably rip up one of my best band shirts."

"She has a thing for band shirts. Her Social Distortion shirt got torn up one time. She was pissed.I think she killed the guy who did it." Cash tossed a roll of gauze to Nolak. "Mason called me, looks like I missed all the fun."

"It wasn't a guy, it was a demon." I hopped back up on the counter, holding my leg up for easier wrapping. "And I killed him because he killed people. A lot of people, I still see that warehouse sometimes when I close my eyes." A shiver ran up my spine and, for a moment, I was back where the demon had killed the men who summoned him.

"Somebody's got a serious hate on for you. You must have really pissed someone off. I mean, more than usual." Cash leaned against the doorway, watching Nolak intently as he mummified my leg with gauze. "I give them high marks for creativity, though. First the magic mind bomb and now a zombie."

"Pffft, they don't even have the balls to come after me themselves and they just made a huge mistake. They took my dog."

7

Stabbing pains shot through my leg every time I moved, making it impossible to relax. Cash and Nolak insisted I get some sleep. An impossible feat, given Conry's disappearance, an hour had passed since Mason talked to anyone and there was no word from my father. A sense of dread settled into my heart.

The healing process was slow and uncomfortable due to some sort of anticoagulant in the zombie saliva. My calf grew back, filling in the missing chunks with new, tender muscle. The gauze had been removed, exposing the first layer of translucent skin covering the sensitive flesh. The slightest brush with the fabric or whisper of air felt like icicles pelting my leg. I laid there for another hour, willing each new layer of skin to knit together.

Unable to sit still any longer, I ventured out of my bedroom and into the kitchen. Cash and Nolak made themselves comfortable at my table drinking coffee and rehashing the day's events. Both heads swiveled around, surprised to find me standing there. I stumbled over to the coffee pot and filled a cup before addressing the frustrated faces in my kitchen.

"Did Mason call?"

"You're supposed to be resting. You're no good to anyone if you're not fully healed." Cash pushed out the empty chair beside him.

"I rested. I won't be running any marathons today, but I'm pretty sure I can manage drinking and talking. What about London and Anderson? You hear anything yet?"

"You barely made it to the coffee pot." Nolak didn't look up from his notes scribbled on the back of a Jesse Wong takeout menu.

"I appreciate your concern, really I do. Put yourself in my shoes for a second. My dog and now my boyfriend are missing. We have no leads on their location and nothing panned out on the dead were or his lawyer. I don't care how jacked up my leg still is, I'm not going to just lie in bed and do nothing."

"So you admit you're still in bad shape." Nolak set the pen down and looked at me. "The skin on your leg is an interesting shade of pink, by the way. You need to sit this one out."

"Cash." I growled his name, not for his attention, more like an advisory warning to intercede.

Nolak didn't do or say anything out of line. In fact, he was a man of few words, which I could appreciate as much as the next girl, but the thread tethering my composure was unraveling.

Laughter mixed with coughing. "Ease up Nolak. She admitted she's still hurt. That is a major development in her personal growth."

Dignified I raised my jaw slightly, until I realized there was a little jab in there somewhere. "I think we can at least agree my house arrest is not working out according to plan."

"Let me guess, you've got a new plan. One that involves storming in somewhere and kicking a lot of ass." Nolak knew me better than I thought.

A wicked smile split my face. "Sort of. First I need to talk to my father."

Cash shook his head, ready to sideline me from any action. I stopped him with one look.

"Somebody put a bounty on my head and a zombie managed to take a few chunks out of me and I'm reduced from Regulator of Salem and the greater Massachusetts area to fragile woman who needs to be covered in bubble wrap and safe guarded by alpha males. I can't do it by myself, but I can hold up my end.

"So before you huff and puff and blow my plans down, hear me out." I waited a breath for their interruption, barreling on when there wasn't one.

"First, we go to Gallows Hill. If anyone can help us find Conry and Mason, it's my father. From there, we pay a visit to the one person in Salem capable of raising a zombie. It's unlikely Graive is involved. The vampires have been waiting for her to screw up. Still, I'd feel better if we could officially rule her out." I took a sip of my coffee and continued explaining my plan.

"Aidan will be here soon with the rest of the team. We split them up. Since he's immune to necromancy, we take him with us. The rest of my crew will handle council business out in Danvers. There's another black coven and a lot of bad magic floating around. I don't like it. Maybe it's connected, maybe it's not. We'll know for sure tonight."

Their dumbfounded stares were a little insulting. I decided to let it slide. Cash and Nolak exchanged glances, shrugged shoulders and nodded their heads. I leaned back in my seat, trying to analyze their bizarre form of sign language. Clueless to the nuances that differentiated one bob of the head from another, I failed to decipher their code. Decisions were made without saying a word, in silent communication honed over years of fighting side by side- on a battlefield and in the pack.

I waited patiently for what seemed like an eternity, but was closer to five minutes before throwing my hands up. "Oh, come on. It's a good plan and you know it."

"What's a good plan? And what happened to your door?" Ryanne was the second person to walk through my wards without setting off a single alarm.

I was fairly certain she meant me no harm, the fact remained my apartment wasn't safe anymore. Too many people knew about me, knew where to find me. I'd have to move. I added that problem to my ever growing list of things to do. Find Conry, find Mason, find and stop whoever is trying to kill me, get new place.

Piece of cake.

Vampirism suited Ryanne well. The alabaster skin tone common among the undead was only a shade or two lighter than her natural Irish complexion. Red hair framed her face, highlighting her green eyes. The soft blush in her cheeks a telltale sign she'd fed recently.

Aidan trained her well. In a few short months, she gained independence most vampires didn't have after a century of undead living. We hadn't spoken since the night she was turned. To say I was surprised to see her standing in my apartment was an understatement.

"Have you devised a plan for our latest assignment already?" Aidan walked in with an air of confidence I'd never be able to pull off, the remainder of our team at his back.

"She's planned a lot more than that," Cash called out from the kitchen.

"What's under the tarp?" Ryanne moved to lift a corner before I swatted her hand away.

In an effort to keep things calm and productive, I chose to ignore a couple of things. Not only was Ryanne uninvited, she wasn't part of the team.

"We've got a lot to cover. Let's get started."Heads turned from the abnormally-shaped mound hidden beneath a blue plastic tarp to the stack of paperwork in my arms. More than one eyebrow rose as I passed out the folders with colored tabs poking out of the sides. "What?"

My team was smart enough to know to keep their heads down and the snickering to a minimum. The last chuckle over my attempt at organization died away once they opened the files, immediately recognizing the dark witches for what they were.

A threat to all of us.

"Blood magic calls to even the strongest earth witch. If we allow it to take root in a neighboring town, it won't be long before Salem is infested."Dre flipped through his file, stopping on the page with a photo of the coven leader.

"I'm glad to see you feel that way, Dre.You'll take point on this one. Head out to Danvers. Observe the coven, see who's coming and going. The Council was clear; no one walks out of there. Not even the familiar. Make sure the leader is on site before you move in."

Dre gave a low whistle. "Hannah Crane? A woman?"

"A very smart, very pretty, very deadly woman. Don't get caught thinking with your dick on this one, Dre. If you come in contact with Crane, put the bitch down."

Aidan sought out Andre Renault for the team ten years ago. A member of the French Foreign Legion in his human life, his passion for military action continued throughout his undeath. He also loved gin. He'd tried on more than one occasion to mix it with blood and juice, which earned him the nickname Dre. He gave up protesting the name when I caught him singing "*Ain't nuthin'but a g thang*." He was an asset and the best choice to lead the team.

"The amount of violence in here, I just wasn't expecting a woman that's all." Dre tapped the folder tucked under his arm.

"Don't be fooled by a set of full lips and soft curves. It's how we got you to eat that apple in the first place. Risqué is our new home base until further notice. Keep me posted."

My team reluctantly followed Dre out of the apartment. I caught more than one glance at the tarp. They weren't stupid. They knew I was in deep shit. I usually was. I gave them their assignment and it wasn't babysitting me. If I could have kept them all with me I would have. Much to my disappointment he world turned whether I was on it or not. Letting blood magic take hold was not an option.

"Aidan, wait up a sec. I need you..."

He amped up the vamp, moving from the broken front door to stand by my side in the blink of an eye. "What, what do you need?" His hand glided up my arm, cupping my face.

"I need you to turn it down." My eyes flicked between the two wolves that walked out of my kitchen on the verge of shifting, to the newbie vampire whose fangs elongated. "You're pumping out a lot of pheromones right now and it's upsetting the rest of my guests."

He let me go and dialed it back. "I'm sorry." He nodded to Cash and Nolak before leaning in to whisper in my ear. "I never thought I'd hear you say those words again. I forgot myself for a moment."

I tried to recall if in fact I'd ever said those words to him while he checked on Ryanne, who no doubt still felt the effects of her maker's pheromone drop.

Pupil dilation was one symptom of over excitement in younger vampires. A common misconception that gave way to the myth all vampires had black eyes. Prior to the Shift -back when others kept to the shadows-information was based on interaction with the very young or the poorly trained.

When raised properly, a vampire learned to control their eyes, fangs and the pheromones that made them so alluring to humans. A human could be in the company of an elder vampire and never know it. Viper fangs with eyes as black as pitch, these were the outlandish legends passed on from the few lucky enough to survive an attack.

Ryanne remained stoic through his examination. Aidan checked her pupils and peeled back her lips to examine her fangs before praising her strength and control. The tenderness in her eyes and his touch left no doubt of their connection. Ryanne wasn't the first vampire Aidan made, just the first he considered family.

"You've only ever had to ask, Maurin. I'm powerless to deny you anything." Aidan hung his head, disappointed in himself for admitting it.

I was about to ask the unthinkable.

"We haven't heard from Mason in hours. I need you to help me find him." His shoulders dropped, my heart and stomach went with them. "It's a long shot. Still, Graive's our best lead right now. And Conry's missing too."

My small, one bedroom apartment shrank down to the size of a shoe box. The weight of everything pressed against me as I awaited his answer.

"When I said anything, rescuing your boyfriend from a necromancer wasn't exactly what I had in mind."

I knew there was a chance he'd refuse to help me find the person who possessed the one thing he wanted and couldn't have - my heart.I'd resolved myself to the possibility of begging when I decided to ask for his help. If it turned out I had to go up against a powerful earth coven and a necro, I needed more than two werewolves. I needed the one vampire immune to necromancy.

"I know I'm asking a lot. Aidan please," I pleaded.

"I'll help you." A sigh of relief escaped me before he laid out his terms. "On one condition."

"So much for being powerless to deny you anything." Nolak earned himself an elbow to the ribs for that. Cash knew as well as I did how much we needed Aidan's help.

"Have dinner with me."

"Aidan, now is hardly the time." Ryanne seemed torn between loyalty to her maker and loyalty to the man who took her in and cared for her when she was a human.

"It is the perfect time. What do you say Maurin? Is the life of your new lover not worth the cost of one evening spent in my company?"

"I don't know if you can afford it." Cash leaned in to whisper in my ear.

"I can't afford not to."

"Then clearly state your terms." Cash moved back beside Nolak, waiting for our deal to be struck.

I silently called Aidan every name in the book for capitalizing on the disappearance of my dog and my boyfriend. "I'll have dinner with you and nothing more."

"Full courses, you're mine for an entire evening."

"Food is the only thing on the menu."

"A date of my choosing."

I looked over my shoulder at Cash. I hoped he'd tell me if I gave too much or countered too little. I got a noncommittal shrug instead. "Fine, one evening of dinner and nothing more on a night of your choosing."

"Agreed. Ryanne, I'm afraid our plans have changed. Something tells me this is not a good night to begin your training as a cleaner. Why don't you return home, order something from Bloody Mary's? Tell Gillian to put it on my tab."

Bloody Mary's, a twenty four hour blood bank and delivery service, opened two new locations last month alone. The blood business was obviously booming. I was surprised to hear Aidan was not only a customer, but had a tab, since he preferred his meals directly from the vein.

The look Ryanne gave me on her way out unsettled me. She seemed genuinely concerned. *About what?* My bargain with Aidan or the quest to find those that were taken from me? To be honest, I was more than a little worried about that part myself.

8

"That's your plan?" Aidan bent over what remained of the zombie, covering his noise from the stench that built up beneath the plastic cover. "Storm the witch house and accuse her of trying to kill you? I admit she had reason to when you were tangled up with her boyfriend. She has what wants. Why now? Why risk the Council's wrath?"

"I'm not storming anything. I just want to talk to her. And I wasn't tangled up with Oberon. I was bewitched." I opened a window to clear out some of the smell.

"Might I suggest a more tactful approach?"

"I'm all ears." A breeze blew the acrid smell up from the floor. "Just please, make it quick because Hey Man is really starting to smell."

"Hey Man?" Aidan pointed to the decomposed body. "I thought you said this was the man from the first floor? Joe, right?"

"For fucks sake! Mike. His name is Mike." Cash replaced the blue tarp. "Have some respect."

"That's what I meant. We can't let Mike just decompose in my living room." I added a little emphasis to his name.

"Invite her over to examine his remains. If she is lying, your wolves will taste it. If she is truthful, you avoid causing offense with unwarranted accusations."

"I suppose we could try it your way."

Graive arrived shortly after I called and explained the situation. She pulled back the plastic, nearly gagging when the foul air wafted up from the corpse. "How long did you say this body has been here?"

"Not long, a few hours maybe." I doubted there was a steam cleaner powerful enough to remove the evidence of Mike's demise from my carpet. It would have to be replaced.

"You're certain? The rate of decay doesn't match your time line. Properly raised, a zombie shouldn't look like this for weeks."

"So we're dealing with a novice? Someone untrained in the art of necromancy?" Aidan watched her push back the bloated lips, revealing the razor sharp teeth I had become all too familiar with.

"I don't think you're dealing with a necromancer at all." She twisted her white hair into a knot at the nape of her neck, before reaching back down to examine the jaw bone. "Hobyah." She sighed, rubbing her hand over her brow.

I cringed at the slimy streak glistening on her forehead from the decay she smeared across it.

"What's a Hobyah?" I went into the kitchen to grab a clean dish towel. "You've got a little bit of Mike on your face." I pointed to the spot on her face and tossed her the towel.

"A Goblin, one that can take on the appearance of any human," she mumbled through the terrycloth. "After it eats them, of course."

"Of course," Cash grumbled.

"So it's safe to assume Maurin's neighbor is dead." Aidan walked circles around the body. "What else do you know about the Hobyah?"

"To be honest, not very much. There's a paragraph, maybe two, in the Key of Solomon warning necromancers of the signs a Hobyah is in your territory. You can see why." She gestured to what was left of Mike. "Once they take on the shape of a human, they burn a lot of power maintaining the illusion. They have to consume flesh at an alarming rate or they'll start decomposing. I've heard some necro urban legends, you know a friend of a friend of a friend's uncle was killed for raising a rabid zombie, when they killed the necro and the zombie didn't die, they realized it was a goblin. They're fae, maybe you should be asking your dad about this instead of me."

"We're headed to Gallows Hill after this. Graive, could you send me a copy of that page from the Key? Maybe it says something else."

Another fae. Son of a bitch.

"Sure. I'll email it to you when I get back to the house." She poured coarse salt around the body and pulled a small dagger from inside her leather trench coat.

After slicing her palm with the miniature blade, she opened and closed her fist, pumping the blood out of the wound as she walked. The white salt crystals turned pink then red as it absorbed her blood. Strange words in a language none of us understood filled the silence as we watched her.

"Just in case." She shrugged her shoulders.

Graive made a circle, trapping the goblin on the off chance it wasn't really dead and tried to crawl out of my apartment.

Necromancers spent their lives with one foot in the world of the living and the other in the world of the dead making their souls immune to the marks of blood magic. She was neither light nor dark. Both ends of the magical spectrum resided in every necro. They were perfectly balanced.

That didn't mean I was entirely comfortable with her powers. Of course I would have been even less comfortable if the hobyah got up and walked away, so I thanked her for her help before she left.

"My car is still at the station. Cash, can you drive?" A familiar jingle caught my attention. "You have the Camaro?" My eyes zeroed in on the keys in Aidan's hand. Damn that vampire, he knew how much I loved that car. "I'll drive." I snatched the keys, stepping over the rubble around my front door.

It was a tight fit with the four of us in the classic muscle car, especially in the back seat where Cash and Nolak were squeezed together. Two normal-sized guys could fit in the back with room to spare, two large werewolves, on the other hand, did not.

"Why are we driving to Gallows Hill? Why aren't you jumping there?" Aidan stilled my hand on the gear shift. "Maurin, why aren't you going into the Between?"

"I promised Mason I wouldn't go alone. If I'm going to break that promise, I don't want to do it here. My wards are down, blood magic is permeating my carpet and Conry's gone." Pain stabbed my heart just saying his name. "No, if I'm going to do this, it has to be somewhere else." I threw the car in reverse and sped out of the lot.

9

I stood on the hallowed ground in Gallows Park. Every blade of grass, the root of every tree surrounding the park,had been fortified with the blood of my enemies, with my blood. The emotions imprinted here were strong enough to feel without a fingerprint or a memory link. The energy recognized me as well. Power swelled the earth beneath my feet, thickened the air around me.

My fingers trailed across the damp air, collecting moisture from the fog as I searched for the thinnest spot in the veil. I wanted my entrance to be as discreet as possible. Power surges in the Between drew too much attention. Until I knew who or what wanted me dead, I had to keep a low profile. Finding a weak spot in the veil meant I used the least amount of power. It was as close to stealth mode as I could get.

I found the perfect place, my fingertips easily slipping into the Between. "See you on the flip side boys." I winked at my friends, an attempt at bravado I didn't feel.

Aidan flashed to my side before I disappeared through the veil. "Take one of us with you. You've done it before. Don't go into the Between alone."

"It could send out a power flare. I can't risk it. My father told me we were connected to this place, he'd know if I entered the Between here."

"Aidan, let her go." The double meaning of Cash's words hung heavily in the air.

"You'll leave immediately if something doesn't feel right?" Aidan said, ignoring him.

"Mason taught me how to sense other fae moving through the Between. I'll know if someone other than my father is there."

I held out hope that I would find Mason there, too. He would never leave me, not with a bounty on my head, not if he could help it. I blinked back the tears threatening to fall at the thought of him injured and incapable of healing himself. *What if he was somewhere I'd never find him, unable to reach out to me?* I forced the thought from my mind.

Aidan trailed a finger along the chain on my neck. "Well there's at least one thing I can thank him for."

My hand flew to the apple wood charm instinctively, catching Aidan's hand instead. Caught off guard again by the sensation of cool metal against my skin and the gentle tug of the weight of the chain against my neck that hadn't been there when I left my house, I didn't see the kiss coming.

Aidan seized the opportunity my bewilderment over the magically appearing necklace provided. He moved in with lightning speed, his mouth landing softly against mine. He aptly moved to the sensitive spot on my neck he had no claim to anymore.

I held back the shudder from his cool breath on my skin, afraid it would only encourage him.

Wolves growled a warning, breaking the moment before it ended in an explosion of passion or rage -which pretty much summed up the kind of relationship I'd had with Aidan.

"Hurry back." Aidan released me before I had a chance to react or formulate a response.

I looked at Cash, held back by Nolak and whispered that it was okay, that I was okay. Aidan didn't know enough about my abilities to understand that keying me up emotionally caused flare ups of energy. To his credit, I didn't know that when we were together. I'd only learned it recently thanks to Mason. He'd taught me how to control it.

Cash knew because he was the closest thing I had to a best friend. He worried about me, it was written all over his face. I reassured him one more time that I was fine.

I shook off the fear that I'd be fighting off reminders of the way Aidan used to make me feel the entire time he was helping me search for the man I had promised my heart to and stepped into the Between.

Time and space worked differently here. The Between was a place where worlds were created and destroyed, the beginning of all possibilities. Hours could pass in minutes or minutes could take hours-it was fae after all. Warmth radiated up my spine through the markings on my back, but the restorative feeling I'd grown accustomed to whenever I slipped behind the veil escaped me.

I sat down, crossing my legs and closed my eyes, concentrating on my father. Normally, my presence would be enough to call him. Keeping your focus on a person or a place was the key to manipulating the Between. There were too many things swirling in my mind to do it properly. Images of my father shifted to images of Conry which faded to images of Mason. Torn over contacting my father or searching for Mason and Conry, I couldn't focus on just one.

Overwhelmed with the need to find them, my thoughts kept slipping to dark places. I crammed a fist in my mouth to stifle the scream building. My heart constricted, shattered into a million pieces as I imagined their torture. I forced the pictures from my mind. I couldn't afford to let my imagination run wild in the Between. I didn't know where they were, much less the condition they were in. If I allowed my fear to impair my abilities I'd never find them. And that was not an option.

I mentally called out to my father. Nothing. I tried again with the same results. I tried Mason. Again, nothing. I slowly drew in more of the Between, careful to avoid any bursts of power that could attract unwanted attention. The more I pulled in, the more it felt off.

Someone moved in the Between, but I couldn't tell if they meant me harm. Convinced I wouldn't be able to track any of the men missing from my life, I refused to take a chance. I threw up my guard and prepared to make my exit.

Blackness stirred in front of me before I could step through the veil. Thick clouds shifted and swirled around something forming inside them. Drawn to the mesmerizing vortex, I peered into the center, recoiling only when the first black feather flitted out. Wings snapped, beaks pecked as the flock dive bombed around me kamikaze style.

I swatted, ducked and finally hit the ground, throwing my arms over the back of my head. "I fucking hate crows!"

"I'd heard that about you." Kellen's voice registered the same moment as his energy. "Of course, I've always found the molmacha to be excellent heralds. Did you know the birth of the first Unseelie heir was foretold by the flock?"

I sat up, pushing my hair back out of my face so he could see the stink eye I gave him. "Did you know the last time a bunch of crows swarmed around me, they turned into a goddess hell bent on killing me? Why are you here Kellen? Where's my father?"

"You wound me, Maurin. You ask as if I have something to do with your father's disappearance."

It was a damn good thing I wasn't standing because that bit of news would have dropped me for sure. "What, what do you mean my father's disappeared?"

"All of the Hunt it would seem."

"All of the Hunt? All of the Hunt, gone?"

"You have an annoying habit of repeating what others say in the form of a question. Are you aware of that? Yes, all of them."

The ground suddenly dropped out from under me. My stomach found a new home in my throat as the sensation of free fall took over my body. The air thinned, each breath becoming a struggle. Pressure built behind my eyes and ears.

"Shall I manifest a paper bag for you to breathe into or are you going to pull yourself to together?" Kellen wasted little time waiting to see if I would snap out of it. "The Between is actually responding to your emotions. As fascinating as that is, I can't say I enjoy these mortal fears you indulge in." He grabbed a hold of my shirt.

I bounced once before landing in a tangled mess at Cash and Aidan's feet when Kellen tossed me out of the Between. "Gone." I fisted a hand in Cash's jeans. "They're all gone."

"She'll be fine. She's back to repeating things." Kellen gripped me beneath my arms and lifted me up. "There isn't that better?"

His placating tone reminded me of my mother's. She said the same thing after giving me a sedative when I had one of my *episodes*, then she locked me in my room until I slept it off. I started wearing gloves after that. Shaking myself free of the memory, I steeled my spine and tried to pull myself together.

"Who's gone?" "What are you talking about?" "Where's Arawn?" Aidan and Cash asked questions in rapid fire succession.

I looked to the only person out on Gallows Hill that had any answers. "Well, Kellen?"

"Members of the Hunt have been disappearing from their outposts. Your father called the Cwnn Anfwnn home. None have returned. He retreated to Otherworld. That was the last I heard from him."

"Has the Council been made aware of this?" Aidan looked at Cash, suspicion in his eyes.

I knew better.

"I have other things to do besides hang around in that den of iniquity you call a council room. I'm informing a fellow member now."

"I seriously doubt anything you've seen beneath Risqué has offended you. In fact, I'm certain you've been spending more time in the old speak easy than you have in Faerie." Cash folded his arms across his chest and glared back at Aidan. "See Fanger, first I've heard of it."

"Now is not the time for you two to start that bullshit again." Aidan and Cash's mutual dislike was legendary. They'd managed to work together on a few council projects without incident. Tensions were high, people were missing and things were spiraling out of control. It was easy to slip back into the familiarity and comfort of their old relationship.

Something whizzed past my ear before I could chastise them further. Warmth spread along my neck as something wet dripped from my earlobe. A hiss escaped my lips when I touched it. I wiped my fingers on my jeans, not surprised to see two red streaks left behind. Cash dropped to his knees, clawing at his back. Something sliced through the air again, too quiet to be a bullet. Aidan stiffened, his body completely rigid as he fell straight back, an arrow protruding from his chest.

"The Dark Guard, Unseelie assassins." Kellen shouted over the arrows raining down upon us.

"The tree line." I pointed to the copse of trees where the arrows seemed to be coming from.

Nolak bolted on all fours after our attackers. His massive paws echoing like thunder in the otherwise silent night as he ran toward the Unseelie.

White lightning struck my left leg, dropping me to my knees. Fatigue overrode the pain, forcing me to a prone position, my leg turned at an awkward angle to keep from driving the arrow deeper. The arrowhead was made of iron. I rolled to my back, panting from the effort it took to move. I struggled to pull it free, my fingers barely able to grasp the thin wood.

"Leave it. The arrow is made to pull free of its tip. We'll have to cut it out."

"Son of a bitch." Cash growled, halfway through his shift. A broken arrow lay at his feet. "Silver, not enough to kill me. Change will force it out." His fangs and the silver burning in his veins made it difficult for him to talk.

I crawled toward Aidan, the arrowhead cutting through muscle with each painful movement. With one hand on his shin, I reached out for Cash's paw with the other. I spindled the Between, pulling in as much as I could hold in preparation to jump us the hell out of there. I'd done it before, moved the three of us, when they were beating the crap out of each other in a bar at my sister's wedding. It was messy and exhausting. We landed in a heap on my living room floor with me on the verge of throwing up on my carpet. With all three of us injured, it'd be a miracle if we didn't get stuck in the Between. I hated to leave Nolak behind, but I couldn't risk calling out and alerting the Dark Guard of my attempt at escape. He was an alpha in his own right, powerful and smart. I had to trust that he'd get himself out, that we'd find him later.

"Wait." Kellen whispered something in elvish, stirring the wind.

I'd learned to fear his power the night he force fed it to me, jumping me from Risqué to Winter Island against my will. I stayed out of the Between for weeks after that, afraid he'd be there. Mason taught me how to sense other fae with the ability to manipulate the Between. There weren't many of us. Kellen was the strongest, next to my father, and the only one besides Arawn who could pour his power into you and control your jump.

According to my father, it didn't have to hurt, in fact it could be quite enjoyable. Kellen was just a sadistic fuck who got off on other people's pain. He still scared the hell out of me, despite only hurting me that one time. We'd developed an understanding, he didn't cause me pain and I didn't sick my father on him. Kellen feared little else besides Arawn and his Wild Hunt.

A fact that had me questioning the uninjured fae helping us. Why hadn't he been hit? How did he reach me in the Between so fast? My father was the only one constantly tuned into this place in anticipation of my call. How did Kellen know to be here? I slowly scooted closer to Aidan and Cash, careful not to draw the fae's attention as I tightened my grip on them. He'd no doubt follow us, but we'd be out of the Dark Guard's reach.

Arrows pierced the ground to my right. I turned to see what the Unseelie were shooting at. Shock stopped me from making my escape with a vampire and wolf. The illusion Kellen created was like nothing I had ever seen. I watched as his glamour unfolded. Perfectly solid, three dimensional recreations of the four of us drew the Guard's fire, while we became invisible behind some sort of magical camouflage.

"I see the doubt in your eyes. If the Guard is after you, skepticism is wise. Rest assured I am on your side. I can't hold this for long. I'm strong, but my power is finite. We need to move. I am not as familiar with this plane as I should be. We need some place safe to remove the iron, silver and rowan wood from your bodies."

"If I think of the place you can jump us there?"

"Yes, if you hurry."

I focused all my energy on conjuring the image of where I wanted Kellen to take us in my mind. Grey skies replaced dark of night, emphasizing the emerald ground. Air tainted by city was blown away by the rich scents of farmed earth. Stone replaced the grass beneath us as fire from the massive hearth warmed my skin. We arrived safely at Mason's home outside Kilkenny.

The sensation of being home, of being close to him, overwhelmed me. I collapsed on the rug in front of the fireplace as Kellen rushed to close the shutters, shrouding the room in darkness. I'd forgotten about the time difference when I chose this place. Safety was my only concern and I knew there were wards surrounding this place older than Mason. His wards fell back at my apartment. For some reason, I felt certain the ones here would hold.

"Thanks." I nodded toward the windows and then Aidan. "And for back there. We wouldn't have gotten out of there without you."

"You could have jumped, you're strong enough. I followed because I feared they would follow you without the glamour. And with all three of you fighting toxins, well they'd make short work of finishing you off."

Cash circled the rug a few times before curling up next to me. The air shimmered around him as he pulled on pack magic to cleanse the silver from his body. A couple hours in his wolf form and he'd be good as new. I ran my fingers through his fur, whispered a few soothing words over his whimpers of pain and no doubt worry for Nolak.

"We need to get that out of Aidan's chest. Any ideas?"

"I planned to cut it out the same way as yours."

"He'll need blood."

"Let's hope he's strong enough to hunt when he wakes then because he'll get none from either of us. Your days of letting vampires gnaw on your flesh are over."

"It was one vampire, just Aidan. God, does everybody know?"

"Yes. I cannot speak for the Court of Shadow but my Queen has overlooked the discretion because you weren't aware of the danger."

"Great. Thanks. Let's just cut the arrow out of him, okay?" I grumbled, unhappy that apparently all of Faerie had been gossiping about me.

"We'll tend to your wounds first."

"No, help Aidan. The arrow is so close to his heart. He could die."

"Then I suggest you take care not to jostle him about. Right now, he's simply immobilized, like a coma. As for you, the iron is already breaking down inside your body. If I don't remove the arrowhead now, it will spread through your circulatory system and you will die."

"Okay, me first."

Holding still proved impossible with Cash breathing dog breath in my face and Kellen prodding around inside my thigh. You'd think the weight of Cash's wolf on my chest would have held me in place. I managed to buck him off when Kellen's blade scrapped bone.

"Tell me about the Dark Guard. I need to think about something besides what you're doing to my leg. Why were they in Salem?" I ground out through clenched teeth.

"I honestly don't know. Perhaps they were looking for your father."

"Why? And why were they trying to kill us?"

"Arawn rules over a place between the courts. He is neither light nor dark. There have always been those that wish to wield that power for their own gain. To control the Wild Hunt, one could eliminate all houses that stood against them."

"So it's about politics?"

"With the fae it's always about politics. Tell me, why this place? The possibilities were endless and you chose to send us here. Why?"

"I don't know. It was the first thing that popped into my head."

Satisfied he removed all the iron, Kellen flushed the wound and dried off my leg. "I think there's more to it than that."

"My place isn't safe, I needed a home base, somewhere I've been before." It was more than that. I wanted to be close to him. While his apartment in Salem had memories, nothing held a candle to this place. He stole my heart in this room, in front of this fireplace.

"And Mason is home to you, isn't he?"

"Yes." And I would tell him, as soon as I found him.

"Interesting. And you haven't mated?"

97

"That's none of your goddamned business. I can heal the rest on my own, thanks." I jerked my leg back, wincing when the cut on my leg protested.

"If you had claimed him, you would be able to find him. It is one of the benefits of mating."

I tried to figure out a way to ask Kellen if mating meant sex or something else without looking like an idiot while he removed the rowan wood arrow from Aidan's chest. If sex was the tie that binds, locating Mason just got a whole lot easier.

"So you know, Mason and I, we've you know..." Smooth, that was the only word to describe what I just said.

"You consummated your relationship. You never claimed him, never marked him as yours, and now your fear will be his undoing."

Once again, my friends and I were ass deep in trouble and sinking further by the minute. I'd played by the rules, taken a back seat and followed orders. Fat load of good it did me. People I cared about were still hurt.

Aidan woke up looking worse for wear and sparing me from more of Kellen's ominous warnings. He needed to feed. He'd never make it wait until sunset when he could venture out on his own. Cash had already changed back and grabbed some of Mason's clothes to replace the ones shredded when he shifted. "I'll go."

"You sure? I can go." *Say yes, say yes*, I willed him to answer. The iron arrow was gone, but I felt queasy from the exposure. I knew I wasn't up for a field trip.

"Yeah, I got it. You should eat something, too. You going to stick around for a while," Cash asked Kellen. Worry for Nolak weighed heavily on him. It was written all over his face. Nolak was more than a pack mate or second in command. He was Cash's best friend, his brother. He needed a distraction, even one as small as fetching blood for Aidan.

"I can wait for you to return. After that, I must speak with my queen."

"I won't be long. Try not to eat the fae, Fanger."

Aidan walked Cash to the door, giving him directions to the nearest blood bank. None of us felt comfortable calling in a donor or using the delivery services. No one knew we were here and it needed to stay that way until we were all running on at least fifty percent.

I made my way to the kitchen in search of something to eat. My appetite disappeared the same time the three most important men in my life did. Still, I needed food to fuel my body if I wanted to heal. I grabbed the brie and a bottle of water out of the fridge, surprised at how well-stocked the house was for how little time Mason had spent here lately. I promised him we'd start splitting our time between here and Salem. As expected, I failed to make good on it. I grabbed an apple out of the fruit bowl, a box of crackers from the pantry and a knife out of the block and piled everything on top of a little cutting board. I swallowed a helping of stupidity with each bite of fruit and cheese I took, washing it all down with water and a whole lot of regret.

Mason never said anything about mating and the benefits that came with it. He never pushed me to commit to more than I was comfortable with. I wished he had. I wished he'd forced me to tell him I loved him back at the station because if something happened to him and I never got the chance to tell him how I felt, I'd never forgive myself. I didn't care if he knew it, he deserved to hear me say it. My food threatened to make its way back up at the thought of Mason in pain, maybe dying, without me ever telling him that he meant as much to me as I did to him. Sick to my stomach, I pushed the cutting board away and nursed the bottled water.

"You need to eat more than fruit and cheese. Let me fix you something." Aidan opened the fridge and leaned in, examining its contents.

"You can't cook."

"I remember a few things. I think I could manage an omelet."

"I'm fine, really."

"You're hardly fine. We'll find them, Maurin. I promise."

I gave him a half-smile and rubbed my eyes to keep the tears welling up from falling. "Don't make promises you can't keep. We don't even know where to look."

"Then we'll start at the beginning and we won't stop until we find them. You asked for my help and, right now, that means holding you up, not letting you get discouraged."

"Thank you, Aidan." I smiled weakly. It held a warmth that wasn't there before.

"I've only ever wanted your happiness, Maurin. Even if it isn't with me. That'll be Cash with my dinner."

"All my super skills and I still didn't hear him." I didn't know how to respond to the part about my happiness with someone else, so I just left the words hanging between us.

Aidan tapped the side of his nose with his pointer finger. "I smelled him." He gave me a little wink and went to let Cash in. "At least try to eat something else, a little protein maybe."

I chuckled at Aidan's crack about smelling Cash, and shoved another cracker in my mouth. Aidan loved to rib the wolf about smelling like a dog. I needed that, to laugh, something to ward off the sadness that made its way into my heart since the disappearance of the three most important things in my life. I considered myself fortunate to have my friends with me. I wasn't sure exactly what Kellen's role in all this was or what he was doing at Gallows Hill. He'd only helped us so far. I had no choice but to trust him.

10

"We need a plan." My battered friends and I sat around the kitchen table nursing various wounds trying to figure out our next move. I for one felt overwhelmed. "Mason, Conry and my father are missing, people are lining up to kill me, including an Unseelie death squad, and there's a blood coven making a move on Salem. Why does everything happen in threes? Anyone of those is bad enough. This is a trifecta of fucked up proportion."

"We can at least rule out Graive and the Salem coven. So far, everything points to the fae. Well, everything except the blood magic. If you stay on this side of Faerie you've got a fighting chance." Aidan got up to warm another bag of blood.

"We need to go back to Salem. I need to find Nolak." Cash winced when he saw the look on my face.

"I didn't want to leave him. He took off after the Dark Guard. I was afraid to draw more fire calling out for him to come with us."

Cash grabbed my hand. "I know that. I also know how hard it was for you to leave anyone unaccounted for with so many already missing. I can't help you and take care of the pack. I need my second in command, Maurin."

I put my other hand over his, absorbing some of his warmth. "I'd never jeopardize the pack, Cash. I'll take you back to Salem. Find Nolak. Aidan and I can start by retracing Mason's steps. He was supposed to go back to the hospital to get the names of anyone who came in contact with London and his attorney. It's as good a place as any to start at this point."

"I'll see you all safely home before meeting with my queen. One of us should bring Agrona and Kedehern up to speed as well. The Council must be on alert. Maurin appears to be the target, but would be foolish to assume this is solely about her or the fae."

"Thanks, Kellen." I got up and refilled my coffee, needing one last cup before we headed out. I took a sip, leaned back on the counter and tried to think of a place someone could keep Mason and Conry locked up. My gut told me my father wasn't with them. In fact, I had a sinking feeling they were all being held in different locations. Someone wanted to keep us separated. Who and for what purpose?

"So I guess we have a plan. We split up at Gallows Hill."

"I don't think it wise for you to go back there, Maurin. We'll have to part ways here."

"Aidan, we have to go back."

"He's right, Maurin. If the fae were there for you it would be stupid to go back. Kellen can jump me back." Cash swept me up into a bear hug, ready to say goodbye.

It took a moment to take in all the air Cash squeezed out, so I could breathe again. "No, you don't understand. We have to go back. The Camaro."

I'd been driving my piece of crap car again. Mason offered to let me use his truck whenever I wanted. There was just one problem with that. It was impossible for me to drive. Besides, there was only one other car for me and she was sitting alone in the dark, possibly suffering from arrow damage.

"Jeysus woman, you're worried about the dammed car?" Aidan's Irish accent became more apparent the more irritated with me he was.

"I can't believe you aren't. Obviously, I should have gotten her in the divorce." I crossed my arms over my chest and let out a huff of air.

Kellen laughed and laid a hand on my shoulder. "It's good to laugh. Thank you, I needed that. If you're ready,Wolf?"

It never ceased to amaze me how quickly Cash could shift. One minute, he was crushing my lungs in an embrace comparable to a car crusher and the next he was covered in fur and on all fours. He nudged my hand with his head and licked my palm. My fingers brushed through the soft fur along his throat and chest, before scratching him behind his ears. The veil parted enough for one wolf and one fae to step inside. In an instant, they were gone. Cash on the hunt for his second and Kellen to meet with his queen.

An awkward silence filled the space in the kitchen between me and Aidan. He seemed to have something on his mind, something he wanted to say, but couldn't seem to find the right words. He stepped closer, reaching for my hand as I backed up, bumping into the counter. Cornered, I tamped down the fear irrationally setting in. Aidan would never hurt me, not intentionally. *He would kiss you,* a panicked voice in my head screamed a warning. There was no escape from him as he braced his arms on the counter, caging me in. He inhaled deeply through his nose, drawing me into him before resting his forehead on mine. I stood there frozen, afraid any movement would give the wrong impression. His mouth barely inches from mine, if I turned my head in either direction in an attempt to break away, our lips would connect.

"I'm sorry," he whispered, backing away. "My intention was to embrace you, to console you not stalk you across the kitchen like a psychotic ex-lover. You are as intoxicating as ever."

"I know, it's the blood. Listen I..."

"That was your hang up, not mine. You clung to that as a way to move on with the hunter. I simply made it easier for you, showing you the darkness you kept expecting to find the night you walked in on me feeding from Ryanne. I never should have listened to your father. I never should have let you go."

"Aidan please don't do this, not now."

"I just need you to understand, to know how I felt. What I still feel for you."

"You said you wanted me to be happy, even if it wasn't with you. Mason makes me happy."

"I lied."

"I'm sorry for the way things ended. I hurt you, I know that and I don't want to hurt you again. So I'm begging you, please let go of this, of us. Aidan, I love him." He recoiled as if I slapped him. "I think it's for the best if I go it alone after we get back to Salem."

"No. I can't let you put yourself in jeopardy. There are too many people trying to kill you."

"I'll call Amalie. I'll talk to Agrona, she can send someone else. One of us should be focused on the team and the blood coven problem anyway."

"You love him." He shook his head in defeat. "I can't help the way I feel, Maurin. I won't lie and say a part of me doesn't hope to win you back. I will make you a promise. I will not let it interfere with finding your father, Conry and even the hunter again. Despite what Kellen says, I'm not worried about other forces because I am convinced it's the fae. I know it's all connected to you somehow. And I may have lied to you, hell to myself, that your happiness, even with someone else, is all I ever wanted. I would rather see you with the hunter than know you died at the hands of the fae and I could have stopped it. I will see you safe and the safest place for you right now is at my side."

The conversation shook me to my core. I felt like I was saying goodbye again, getting closure on something I thought already closed. Aidan kept picking at the scab. As much as I wanted his help, needed his help because let's face it he was a deadly vampire assassin, I put him in an unfair and impossible situation.

"Let's go look for your family. The bad memories in this house affected more than I anticipated."

Idiot! I silently scolded myself. I could have taken us to Risqué or one of the safe houses the council owned. Once again I didn't think of anyone except myself. This house had become a home, filled with happy memories of time spent here with Mason. It never occurred to me that it held the exact opposite for Aidan.

"I'm sorry. I should have taken us somewhere else. I didn't think."

"You thought of a place that made you feel safe and it worked. You have nothing to apologize for."

He held my hand, unafraid of the trace memories and emotions I could always catch from him. He held his shields firmly in place, blocking any residual feelings from me; his grip tightened, not in the way a lover's might. With a gentle squeeze of my palm, he signaled he was ready to go.

I pulled back the veil, guiding us through as I mentally deconstructed the stone farmhouse and replaced it with the cold concrete and glass of the hospital.

Aidan took over questioning the hospital staff after I shook the woman at the ER registration when she took too long starring at the picture of Mason I pulled up on my phone. No one saw him. He never made it back. We called the morgue when the hospital proved to be a dead end, just in case he stopped there first. No sign of him there either.

"This is driving me bat shit fucking nuts!"

"That's a lovely image."

"I don't even know where to start looking for Conry or my father. And every place we look for Mason is a dead end." My hand connected with the dashboard in frustration as I vowed to never use the words "dead" and "Mason" in the same sentence again.

I cooed soft apologies to the car, it wasn't her fault after all, and I shouldn't be taking my frustrations out on her. The only highlight in the nightmare of an evening was finding the Camaro exactly as we left her at Gallows Hill. Aidan insisted on driving. I'd been annoyed at first, proclaiming that I was perfectly capable of driving. Shaking the sting from my palm, I conceded he was right, I'd probably end up driving us into a ditch.

11

"Where to?" Aidan backed out of the parking space, idling at the exit from the lot behind the morgue.

"Mason's apartment." I ran my fingers through my hair, wincing when they got caught in a tangle.

"You know he's not going to be there, right?"

"Yes." When I didn't say anything else he put the car in gear and took off in the direction of Mason's.

Mason lived in the heart of the city, in an apartment above a little bakery and cafe. I'd never stayed long enough to wake up to just-baked muffins, no matter how many times he tried to tempt me with warm carbs and freshly brewed coffee if I slept over. Things always turned out badly in my,albeit limited, dating experience. I'd vowed to take things slow, do it right this time, that wasn't working out so well either. The sweet smell of confections wafted out to rub my nose in the mornings I could have had if I hadn't been so afraid of getting hurt, too afraid to take what I wanted.

I stared up at the brick building and the two front windows of his apartment, forcing myself to get out of the car. My feet dragged, resisting the walk through the wrought iron gate, down the alleyway to the side entrance for the apartment above. I dug around in my bag for the key Mason gave me. I hadn't used it since the night of our solstice party. I should have told him I loved him.

Aidan stepped up beside me, gently nudging me out of the way. He pressed lightly on the exterior door, the hinges creaking ominously as it swung in. The marks on the door, gouges in the wood from a crow bar forcing it open stood out now that I noticed them. I'd been so busy pining I completely missed them. Time to get my head out of my ass and get focused. I needed to treat this like any other run I've worked. Pretend it wasn't people I loved that I was looking for just another quarry.

That sounded great in theory. Too bad it only lasted about two minutes. I followed Aidan up the stairs to Mason's apartment where his front door, cocked at an odd angle, barely hung on its hinges. Whoever broke in took their time outside, not wanting any passersby to report a burglary in progress. Once inside the hallway and away from prying eyes, they charged up the stairs and busted down the door.

Mason's scent and magical imprint was all over everything. His wards destroyed, his apartment flipped. He'd been here, they took him here and he made them fight for it. I glanced at Aidan. He smiled meekly at the hope in my eyes. I knew Mason wasn't there. I prayed a real clue, the lead we desperately needed, might be. The small creases at the corner of Aidan's eyes, the worry I caught in them told me exactly what he thought happened. Aidan feared we were looking for a body. I refused to believe my hunter was dead.

With my shields completely down, I walked around his apartment careful not to step on anything that had been tossed on the floor. My fingers skimmed every surface, overwhelming me with an onslaught of memories and emotions. I stopped to pick up a silver picture frame off the floor, the one from his desk. The shattered glass distorted the picture underneath, giving it an odd kaleidoscope effect. I knew it well enough to recognize the picture behind the broken glass.

Conry and I fell asleep on the couch watching a Hitchcock marathon. Mason snapped the picture of us curled up together. He'd yet to get a picture of me when I was awake since I hated having my picture taken - every flaw captured for all eternity, the very idea made me want to wretch.

The picture frame was saturated with Mason's memories. The room spun as images and the strong emotions they stirred flooded my mind. Overwhelmed, my knees buckled, before I managed to snag the link hoping it would be a direct connect inside his head. With one hand on his desk to steady myself and the other pressed on the shattered glass, I made my way through the myriad of thoughts.

Mason's link reminded me of a great oak, deeply rooted with smaller roots spreading out in each direction to anchor and nourish the ancient tree. The memory link came to an abrupt end, sharp as if someone cut it. I reached for a small tendril snaking off the side, opening myself up wider to work the older, weaker link. Another dead end. It continued that way, following link after link, moving sideways, backwards, up and down. Not one of them, not a single memory led me to the moments leading up to his disappearance. Not one link opened a live connection inside his mind. The imagery changed, roots spindled into silvery thread. A web formed, with me at its center. Even though it was all in my mind, the connecting links gave a physical sensation of being on a trampoline. I knelt down, feeling the spring from the tension on the lines even though I knew my knees were in fact against Mason's hardwood floor. Like strings on a harp, I plucked the links, following the vibrations, tuning my powers to the frequency of the chord. At the peak of the chime, I stood, arms out to balance against the sway of the web. The sound resonated deep within my chi, stirring some kind of recognition within my own energy. I looked out over the beautiful structure the links shifted into and had a moment of clarity. I was inside Mason's mind and he had successfully cut me off from anything and everything he didn't want me to see. All the memories he gave access to were of me. He surrounded me with every thought, every ounce of love for me that he had. Things were much worse than I thought.

Aidan screamed my name just as the glass from the two front windows overlooking the walking mall and the shops below shattered, pulling me back from the complicated web of links Mason created to keep me from finding him. "We have to go. Now!" Aidan reached out, pulling me up with one hand.

"Is it the Dark Guard?" I headed to the bedroom, stopping short when I realized he wasn't behind me. "Not out the front."

"There's another way?"

"There's a small deck off the bedroom. It connects to the roof." Another bullet whizzed by, grazing my hip as I raced for the back door.

My hand barley turned the knob before my shoulder barreled into the door, the wood groaning in protest. Aidan was hot on my heels, leaping over the two Adirondack chairs taking up most of the tiny deck as I ascended the rickety ladder leading up to the rooftop garden. He lurched himself over the top two rungs, landing in a defensive crouch beside me.

"Now what?"

"Have you ever gone roof jumping?" I didn't bother waiting for a reply. At his age and in his line of work, I knew he had. I backed up to the edge of the roof and sprinted, pushing off to launch myself onto the neighboring roof the second I reached the ledge.

I landed in a tucked position, rolling to lessen the impact. Aidan landed without so much as crunching a single piece of gravel on the old tar roof. The next building was taller, though not by much. I jumped, catching the edge and hoisted myself up and over. Three rooftops remained, two buildings almost the same height and the last building a full story higher. I wasn't too worried about the drop off the last roof given I had a vampire with me. Aidan would help me down because I had no intentions of jumping into the Between with the Dark Guard across the street. We needed to get gone, that meant getting off the roof and into a car ASAP.

"The Guard has repositioned, they're moving, tracking us across the street. We need to get the hell out of here." Aidan looked down the length of the remaining buildings on our side of the street and then across the alley behind us. "Do you trust me?"

"The last time I answered that question I got hit in the head with one of those riot gun bean bags and then arrested."

"I'll take that as a yes." Aidan charged me, wrapping his arms tightly around me as we propelled off the roof, across the alleyway and over the building on the next street, setting off a car alarm when we hit the sidewalk. "We don't have much time. Jump us to Risqué. We'll plan our next move from there."

"No, we need a car. I'm not jumping anywhere if the Guard is around. They're tracking me somehow. I don't want to get trapped with them in the Between, it's too dangerous."

Aidan eyed a Jaguar and was about to break the window when I stopped him. "Something older, something without key fobs or added security and airbags."

I spied an old Wrangler three cars down. "That'll do." After making short work of the plastic zipper window, I reached in and unlocked the door. One yank on the wire harness underneath the steering column and I had all I needed to hot wire the jeep.

"You're quite adept at boosting cars. I had no idea."

His use of the word "boosting" made me chuckle. I never tired of the mix between old and new vocabulary when Aidan spoke. "Until tonight, Matthison was the only one who knew. He didn't just stumble upon me and my gifts. I got picked up for working in a car ring before my eighteenth birthday. I thought my juvie record was scrubbed. It wasn't. I didn't take a trust fund with me when I left home. I've done some things I'm not proud of. That was before SPTF. Matthison found out who I was, what I could do and offered to expunge my records in exchange for working on his team. It didn't earn me any friends in the supernatural community, but it was a good offer."

"We've all done things we regret." His expression darkened, as if he'd drifted to another time and place for a moment. He rubbed his eyes, clearing away some haunted memory I'd never know about. "I'm not sure how your Boy Scout will react to the news of your criminal past. If he doesn't approve, you should know I find this dark and seedy side of you alluring."

I threw the Jeep in gear and pulled away from the curb with a genuine smile on my face for the first time since everything went to hell. I had no particular destination in mind when I turned right onto Federal St. and headed toward North Salem.

Aidan's cell phone broke the rhythmic sound of the off-road tires humming along the asphalt. "Report, Andre."

I spared a glance his direction. From the firm set of his jaw and telling twitch, I knew it was bad news. "What's happened?" My eyes were back on the road, but Aidan and Dre's conversation had all of my attention.

"How fast can you get us to Danvers?"

"Twenty minutes. What's going on?"

"You heard her. We'll be there in twenty. Don't move in until we get there."

"Aidan, so help me God, if you don't tell me what's going on..."

"Conry is in the witch house."

"The blood coven has my dog?" Aidan grabbed the wheel, righting us back on the road, narrowly missing a car in the opposite lane. "They are so fucking dead."

12

We met up with our team at the edge of the property. A small cottage with shaker siding and shingled roof sat in the middle of a decayed lawn, evidence of the foul magic practiced inside. Under the new ownership the quaint home rapidly deteriorated into squalor. Shutters hung at odd angles, the shrubbery suffered from some sort of blight. Every spell cast in that house took a toll on the surrounding grounds.

Dre moved up beside me. "We've been waiting for the old crone to show herself. She hasn't come back to the house. Jacobs spotted the Cwnn Anfwnn through his scope right before I called you. There was no sign of him before then. No one's been in or out of the house since we arrived."

"Where's Jacobs now?" I wanted a full report. I wanted to know what condition Conry was in.

"Over there." Dre pointed to a boxwood on the left of the house.

All I saw was the bush. Covert didn't begin to describe our team. Dre pulled out a small clicker from his pocket, to anyone outside the cleaning crew, our signals might be mistaken for crickets. A slightly more advanced version of the clicker system used during World War II, we'd taken to using them on runs when our com systems wouldn't work, like in a highly concentrated magical area. Given the lack of vegetation and wildlife, I feared it might give away our location. We all waited for a flood light, porch light, hell, even a flashlight. When nothing stirred inside the house or out, Jacobs made his way over to us.

"What did you see? How's Conry?" I grabbed his arm hoping, praying, for good news.

Jacobs glanced at Aidan, sadness warred with anger on his face. "They've got him chained up. Been performing some kind of bloodletting."

Over the months we'd worked together, the whole team came to look at Conry as a pet. He'd been our mascot, one that could rouse our spirits while ripping out the throat of our enemy. I wasn't the only one out for vengeance tonight.

I cracked my knuckles, eager to dish out some payback. "They have a hostage, they are actively engaged in blood magic. You have a new objective, Jacobs. Clean the scene."

"Yes ma'am." With a glint in his eye, Jacobs moved silently through the yard, bringing our team up to speed.

"You have any daggers on you?" Dre handed me two daggers and a 9mm with a saltwater clip. I checked the safety and shoved the gun in the waistband of my jeans, hissing when the cold metal scrapped against the bullet wound on my hip. Blood still seeped where the iron slug grazed me. Aidan lifted my shirt and tugged at my pants trying to get a look. I swatted his hands away. "It's nothing. I'm fine, just focus."

"You're not healing, that's hardly nothing." Aidan scowled.

"The Dark Guard used iron. It takes longer to heal. I'm fine, really."

"If you're sure."

"I'm sure about making every one of those black witches pay for bleeding my dog."

"I'd say she's fine." Dre gave Aidan a stiff pat on the back before moving in on the house. We stayed on his six.

A hush fell on the group as we closed in on the coven. Hand signals replaced words, each step softer than the one before, the crush of dead grass barely a whisper in the night. Time slowed to a crawl, an eternity passed before the first salt grenade shattered through the window, exploding in a deafening roar of water and shrapnel. Whatever sacrifice the coven planned for the night was contaminated. Dousing a magical area weakens or erases the spell. Everything happened in a blur after that as time rushed up to meet us and then sped on.

Glass rained down as my team burst through window after window. Dre stood on the left side of the door, Aidan on the right. I kicked hard under the doorknob, once, twice before wood splintered and the door swung in. They moved in, Dre first followed by Aidan, sweeping out to each side clearing the room. I stepped in behind them, trying not to breathe in too much of the sulfur, smoke and salt air. It was a noxious combination.

Carpet squished beneath my feet as I moved through the small living room, a mixture of blood and water gushing around my boots. My team made quick and easy work of the witches in this part of the house. Drenched with salt water, their magic was ineffectual, most weren't trained in hand to hand combat or evading a bullet. Conry was nowhere in sight. In the chaos of storming the house he'd been moved, most likely to the basement. There was an old storm cellar door around back. I signaled for Jacobs to check it out and motioned the others forward into the back rooms.

The floor shook violently beneath my feet just before it opened up. I fell, landing hard on the concrete floor, the air in my lungs rushing out. Electricity charged the damp basement, crackling wildly. A powerful witch hid in one of the dark corners, readying for an attack. An explosion rocked the side of the house blowing out the storm door. I caught sight of the witch bolting from the back of the house. She'd run into Jacobs outside. He'd take care of her.

Aidan and Dre bent over the hole, peering down to see if I was okay. I waved to let them know I was fine and pushed myself up into a seated position. Magic stirred again in the pitch black corners of the basement, pressing in on the circle of light in the middle of the room. Something dark and deadly, different than the witch.

A soft, sweet and metallic scent caught my nose. Blood. The altar room. They drained Conry upstairs and performed their magic down here. I scooted into the center of the light shining down through the hole above me, pointing to the furthest corner of the room. I looked up, making sure Aidan and Dre understood what I meant, when something clamped down on my ankle and dragged me into the darkness.

I hadn't meant to scream, but the bear trap-like mouth that bit down on my leg surprised me, not to mention hurt like hell.

"Son of a bitch." Aidan swore, his voice rising above the last of the scuffles upstairs. He dropped down through the hole. "Maurin, don't move."

I recognized the seriousness of his tone. With his heightened sight, he was able to see what gnawed on my ankle. "It's not a black dog is it?"

I'd wrestled with more than one hell hound and was fortunate enough to walk away. They were viscous, poisonous beasts that I had no desire to fight again. I'd barely survived the bite. I waited for the rush of fever, a telltale sign their venom coursed through your veins, making its way to your brain inducing vivid hallucinations. When nothing happened, including further attack from the beast, I bowed my head back looking at Aidan. "Tell me what it is and which direction to swing so I can stab it. My fucking ankle hurts, Aidan."

"It's Conry."

"Where?" A sob broke free from my throat. "Where is he? I can't see him!" My sudden outcry of emotion seemed to upset whatever had ahold of my leg.

It shook me like a pit bull playing tug of war with a toy rope. Instinct took over when the pain became too much. I slashed out with the dagger in my left hand. Aidan cried out for me to stop, to be still. I heard him yell Conry's name one more time as my blade connected with the soft underbelly of the thing biting me. It let go, whimpering as it lay bleeding on the basement floor. Aidan rushed over, not to check my injuries, to see to the beast that attacked me. He dragged it back beneath the light, which to my horror illuminated a familiar white coat.

"Conry!" I scrambled over to my beloved guardian, unwilling to believe he was my attacker until I saw the dagger protruding from his stomach. "Oh my god! What did they do to you? What have I done to you?"

Blood, my blood, stained his mouth, his eyes flat and filmy. Slick, black fluid coated his underside. The coven had been draining Conry of his powerful fae blood and replacing it with something else. Terrified I'd lose him to the transformation from the foul magic, I pumped all of the Between I'd spindled in my chi into my protector. It was my turn to play the savior. He'd rescued me so many times I would give every ounce of my energy to save him. It wasn't enough. His eyes closed and his breathing slowed. He wouldn't survive the night if I didn't take him into the Between.

Aidan could see the wheels turning in my mind. He knew my plan before it had fully formed. "Not here. Let's get him outside, get you both to the edge of the property before you jump. I don't know why, but I don't think you should tap into anymore of your magic until we're away from this place."

I hated to admit it because I didn't want to wait another second to fix Conry. Aidan was right. Something besides blood magic tainted the ground around the house. Dre called down that the house was clear. There was no sign of the crone who'd been leading the coven.

If Jacobs didn't kill her, she'd make her presence known after tonight. We decimated her followers, she would regroup and seek revenge. I wondered if she knew what Conry was and had a bigger part to play in all this, or if Conry had been given to the coven by the person who stole him from me. It didn't matter either way. The coven was shut down and I had my guardian back. I just had to heal him.

Aidan scooped Conry up, gingerly placing him over his shoulder as he hoisted himself out of the basement. Dre, in the prone position at the edge of the hole in the floor, reached down to help me up. I jumped, clasping a hand around his forearm as he pushed himself back with his other arm. I had a hand on the floor, about to pull myself the rest of the way out when I caught sight of something on the makeshift altar. An athame. One that used to belong to a witch who tried to kill me.

"Dre send Jacobs down to retrieve the small sword on the altar. Burn the house when he's clear."

"Jacobs is dead."

I looked over at Jasmina, a fire witch who handled all our burn jobs and now had the miserable task of telling us one of our team members died. "What?"

"He ran into a powerful witch outside, didn't stand a chance. The death curse hit him before he even got a shot off."

"I'm going to kill Mahalia for this. Her time with the fae will seem like a trip to fucking Disney World compared to what I'm going to do to her. Get the athame, burn the house and go with the others to Risqué. Aidan and I will be there soon."

Aidan gingerly handed Conry over to Dre before grabbing my arm and turning me toward him. "What makes you think it's Mahalia? She couldn't have escaped the Seelie prison. It's never been done."

"Just because no one has done it before doesn't mean it can't be done. It's her, trust me."

We followed Dre to the edge of the property where he set Conry down on the first patch of green grass. The apple wood charm on my neck flared when I knelt down beside my dog. Alarmed by the jewelry's reaction to Conry, Aidan reached for my necklace, blistering his skin on the silver. It glowed even brighter when I pulled the dagger from Conry and held a hand over the wound. I started to pull on the veil, wrapping it around us so I could heal my guardian, when a hand rested on my shoulder.

"Allow me. My queen wishes to speak with you." Kellen pulled us through the Between before I could say anything. Aidan and Dre, left behind at the witch house, were no doubt furious if not totally confused as to why Kellen would be whisking me and my dying dog off to Faerie court.

The familiar and comfortable grey of the place between places enveloped us. Kellen set Conry down on the ground, conjuring a medical kit out of thin air. Impressed with his skills in the Between, I watched him pull out supplies from the worn leather satchel. It never occurred to me to create things instead of places here. I've called the Retaliator to me on more than one occasion. It answered because it is a powerful fae relic. I hadn't manifested a new one. Kellen created items at will the same way I created a location. Overwhelmed with the endless possibilities of this revelation, I brought my attention back to Kellen and my dog.

"What are the gloves for?"

Kellen slipped on the second black leather glove. "It looks like they replaced most of Conry's blood with that of a gobyah. I don't want to come in contact with the tainted blood. It's extremely potent and infectious. The witch was minutes away from completing the transformation."

I looked down at my hands, checking for any sign of infection. They looked the same as they did when I woke up, a little calloused from weapon work and in need of some lotion. Satisfied I wasn't going to turn into some form of a viscous goblin with an appetite for human flesh, I asked the question weighing on my mind. "You mean Mahalia?"

He cursed in a language I assumed was elvish as he continued to work on my dog. "When did you realize it was her?"

"When did you realize she wasn't in your prison anymore?"

"She escaped a month ago."

"A month ago? You've known she was gone a month and you didn't think to mention it to anyone?" If he hadn't been in the middle of saving Conry, I would have kicked his ass. "I can't believe she's been missing a month and you didn't tell me."

"Watch yourself, half-breed. I don't answer to you. Unless of course you woke up with a crown upon your head and now sit upon the Throne of Light? No? I didn't think so."

"You sit on the Council. You answer to the other members. They have a right to know."

"What makes you think they don't? You're the Regulator, an enforcer, a hired hand. Do you think that somehow entitles you to know all the goings on of the Council? Let me be the first to inform you, you are mistaken. You have been given far too much rope and have come close to hanging yourself with it on more than one occasion. You are useful, an important weapon in our arsenal. It does not mean you are entitled to know every detail."

"She tried to kill me. Not just kill me, to put me in a circle, tried to banish me with a demon to one of the nine gates of Hell in the hopes he'd kill me when we got there. I'm afraid to step foot in Other World because there are still demons who would love to hurt me for killing the Afrit. I think that entitles me to a little information, like if she's fucking escaped."

His hands stilled above Conry, his shoulders rising before the heavy sigh. "I am sorry I lost my temper. This whole situation is infuriating. Perhaps we should have told you, all of us."

"You're right, you should have."

"And now that you know? What will you do with this information?" His nimble fingers probed and prodded the stab wound as he watched the flow of black blood turn red. He worked the Between, weaving layers as if on a loom until a fine mesh bandage appeared. He placed the patch on Conry, pressing gently until it was absorbed into the gash.

"I sure as hell wouldn't have sat around all this time waiting for her to finish what she started in that warehouse all those months ago."

"Your guardian will be fine."

Conry's eyes flickered open, searching wildly for something. His name left my lips in a song the way a mother soothes an injured child. The muscles in his face relaxed as he recognized my voice, his breath escaping in an exhausted huff as his eyes settled on me. Satisfied we were safe, he stopped fighting his drooping lids and let the healing sleep take him.

"Thank you, Kellen." I continued to whisper sweet words to my boy while I stroked his back.

Eye to eye and side to side, Kellen noticed my necklace for the first time. "It's interesting how fae relics seem to be drawn to you. Careful how many you collect. That much power attracts attention." His fingers brushed the charm dangling from my neck, the metal flaring at his touch.

"Do you know what it does? Mason never told me."

"It grants the wearer safe passage through Faerie."

"Why wouldn't I have safe passage? My father is lord of Other World and I'm fae. Why would this relic find its way to me?" Of all the ancient magical fae items I could have acquired, why couldn't it be something a little more powerful, a little more deadly? There were lots of people trying to kill me.

"Perhaps someone worried a time would come when your halfblooded nature wouldn't be enough to get you in and out of Faerie in one piece. Or perhaps your power called to it. One never can tell with these things."

Headed into the fae Court of Light, his warning didn't elude me. The grey shifted, transforming into a great hall. Huge columns were erected out of the nothingness that surrounded us only a moment ago. Arched ceilings appeared above us stretching down to meet the white marbled walls. Etched window glass in gilded frames dimmed the light beaming in from outside, while music from a harpsichord mixed with the angelic voices of a small choir, trickling down from a balcony above. Saint Peter and the pearly gates were the only thing missing from the celestial picture forming before me. Had some unsuspecting human wandered here, mistaking it for Heaven, or was the imagery of this place one of the things to survive the conversion of pagans? Either way, I admit to being awed by the glitz and grandeur of the Court of Light.

"Oh, this isn't the Court of Light, dear. This is the Hall of Illusion, entrance to either court,Light or Shadow, depends upon the position of the sun and moon in the sky. Fortunately for you, Kellen brought you here while the sun is at its highest point in Faerie."

I turned, blinking from the sparkling light coming off the woman speaking to us. The flowing gold fabric of her gown created a disco ball effect, soft light from the windows refracted off the crystal beadwork sending small globes glittering around the room. My hand instinctively went up to shade my eyes.

"My apologies." With a snap of her fingers the light show dimmed. All that remained was the woman, her beauty no less blinding. "I am Queen Tianna. Walk with me, Maurin." She looped her arm through mine and led me around the great hall. "Your life is in constant turmoil child, a state to which you have adapted well, but this may be too much even for you. Your guardian has been returned to you. Sadly, your father and lover are still missing."

"Congratulations, by the way. No other woman has managed to ensnare the hunter. He was meant only to teach you. Your father is quite the matchmaker. There hasn't been a mated pair within the Wild Hunt since your parents. If I didn't know better, I'd think he was assuring he had a successor. Your reign would be quite remarkable I think. Of course, you'll have to find them for that future to unfold."

She led us around the room while I processed what she said. Fae often talked in circles, leaving you to fumble through their verbal maze, a kernel of truth hidden in poetry or song. A warning buried beneath beautiful words. Kellen kept watch over Conry while we strolled the Hall of Illusion, leaving me with the feeling that we weren't exactly welcome guests or free to leave of our own accord.

"I could help you find them, your father and the hunter. It's clear that someone within the Court of Shadows helped the witch escape. It would be a fair assumption that someone within the king's court is also responsible for your missing men."

"And what would it cost me? No offense your highness, I don't think I can afford the kind of help your offering."

Her grip tightened on my arm, fingertips digging into my bicep. For a moment I saw her true nature, cold, calculating and deadly, before the gorgeous facade slipped back into place. Fae are not the cute little Faeries in children's cartoons or storybooks. They can be wickedly cruel creatures, as dangerous as they are breathtaking. Especially in the Court of Light. Especially when it came to royalty. You don't hold the throne as long as Tianna with just sunshine and daisies. No, there was a trail of blood hidden beneath the train of her dress leading right to the crown.

"Perhaps you would be doing me a favor by capturing and returning my prisoner. Alive or dead, I leave that up to you."

"I think it's for the best if I continue on my own. If things work out favorably for both of us, great. If not, I don't have to worry about someone else trying to kill me." I slipped my arm out of hers, refusing to rub the spot where her nails no doubt left red crescent moons in my skin, and walked over to Conry and Kellen.

Kellen's eyes were wide with shock and something else, concern maybe. No one refused the queen. Ever. Only time would tell if I survived my decision. He looked beyond me, over my head at Tianna. Something passed between them, the smallest movement of his head telling her no. I felt her behind me, but refused to let my fear control me. I wouldn't turn to see if she had a knife ready to plunge into my back. I knelt next to Conry, nuzzling him and whispering that it was time to go home. His tongue ran along my cheek a moment before he sat up, alert and ready to go. I held his muzzle in my hands; looking into the depths of his eyes, I knew he was back, the effects of Mahalia's blood magic completely gone. Only then, when I was certain we were able to leave did I look at her. Kellen probably interpreted this as disrespect. I knew the queen would see it for what it was, a sign that while I may be fae, I was not of her court and I would not be tricked into vowing allegiance to her crown. She would not get control over my father, the Wild Hunt or Other World through me.

"Tha... You've been very hospitable." I caught the thank you before it could become a favor. Never thank the fae, no matter what. You'll owe them if you do. I'd learned that lesson when dealing with a fae who runs an oddities shop in town. Oberon schooled me on the finer points of fae courtesies, something I would have learned as a child had I not been raised by Norms. A wicked grin split Kellen's face, they'd almost had me despite my posturing. "I'll let you know if I change my mind."

Questions swirled in my mind as the veil swirled around me and Conry. Could the Court of Shadows be behind Mahalia's escape? It seemed more and more likely. No one, not in any legend or lore, walked out of a fae prison on their own. What did they stand to gain from kidnapping my father and Mason, or killing me? Were they even still alive? Was control of the Hunt really that important? I needed some answers and fast.

We arrived in the woods a few feet from where Kellen jumped us. Aidan and Dre stood on the spot where we left them. A quick glance at my watch showed only a few seconds passed out here while I was in the Hall of Illusion. Conry sprinted ahead of me, pouncing around their feet. I was suddenly rushed by two very relieved vampires, my guardian happily trotting behind them.

"Damn he's fast. Aidan and I tried to stop him. You just slipped through my fingers. You were just gone." Dre had yet to witness a jump. Until I disappeared with Kellen, he believed nothing was faster than a vampire.

Aidan pawed at me, gently turning me around checking for injuries before crushing me in a hug. I tapped him on his shoulder, my complaints about lack of air muffled against his chest. "You just left. I know he took you to Faerie. I wasn't sure you'd come back. How long were you there?"

"An hour maybe, including the time we spent in the Between while he healed Conry. I wasn't quite in Faerie. I didn't make it further than the hallway."

"The Hall of Illusion? The queen left the Court of Light to meet a half-blood like you in the foyer? That's a bit strange don't you think?" Dre pried Aidan off me to give me a hug of his own, involving more claps on the back and less caressing than the one I just received.

"Very. What did she want, Maurin?"

"She offered to help me find my father and Mason. Not before she admitted Mahalia escaped and pointed more than one finger in the direction of the Court of Shadows."

"What were her terms?"

Aidan already knew the answer to Dre's question. "She didn't ask for them."

"I didn't have to, it was fealty to the crown. I won't tie my father or the Hunt to any court. We'll find them on our own."

"And how do you propose we do that?" Dre stubbornly crossed his arms over his chest, willing me to dazzle him with my planning prowess.

Aidan pressed his palms into his eyes, groaning a little. "She means to question the Dark Guard."

I slipped my right hand in the veil, calling the Retaliator to me. The blade hummed when the hilt hit my hand. I pulled my sword out, swinging the deadly blade, one of the few items that could kill any immortal. "Shouldn't take too long to get the information I need."

13

We didn't have to wait long for the Dark Guard to catch up to us. I'd slipped in and out of the Between twice in a matter of minutes. Not to mention someone within the Court of Light would have sent word of my visit. The fae were notorious for spying and other acts of treason if it meant they'd get closer to the crown. Honestly, I expected better from the king's assassins. Two vampires, a half-blood and a Cwnn Anfwnn waiting in the woods outside of a burning house devoid of life or magic should have seemed suspicious. They moved in because we allowed them to. Where they previously outnumbered us and held the element of surprise, this time we met them on our terms and were equally matched. Four seasoned killers slipped in beside Aidan and Dre. Small, rowan wood spears- fixed on a rotating ring slipped over the middle fingers of the Dark Guard- were pressed against their jugulars.

Aidan gave me a wink and we sprang into action. My vampire teammates spun at lightning speed, taking two of the fae by the throat. They needed to feed and we really only needed one of them conscious. Immortality meant a vampire couldn't kill a fae just by draining their blood. Wild magic kept them alive, while they remained in a comatose state until all their blood regenerated. Conry took down the third as I pinned the fourth to a tree, the tip of my sword pressed against his chest. Once Dre and Aidan finished their meal, I started questioning the guard.

"Where is the rest of your team? There were at least eight of you back at the apartment." Completely cloaked in black, from foot to face, I almost missed the small shake of his head. I knew the information wouldn't come easily. "Do you want to spill your guts or should I?" I moved the Retaliator to his stomach.

"I don't think he's familiar with the saying. Believe it or not, the Dark Guard don't spend a lot of time this side of Faerie. You should just give the other two to the vampires as well. They would offer you no quarter."

"What are you doing here, Kellen?" My heart pounded, rattling in my ribcage from adrenaline and anticipation of the information I could get from the guardsmen. I didn't need interference from him or his queen.

"The Court of Light offers you its deadliest warrior to aid you in your search." He half bowed before returning to his arrogant stance.

The Dark Guard's eyes widened with Kellen's declaration even as I shook my head no and reminded him of my refusal. The king's guard spit in my face, muttering a curse in a language I didn't understand. Kellen laughed at the fae on the deadly end of my sword while he ruined any chances of getting information from the Unseelie with one sentence. If word got back to the King of Shadows that Kellen was helping me I was as good as dead. I allowed two fae to become vampire food - an atrocity in the eyes of both courts and one I would no doubt stand trial for. The possibility of a new prisoner in Mahalia's cell loomed before me. Killing them to prevent one falsehood from reaching the Court of Shadows? As a half-blood I'd be executed immediately. There'd be no need for a bounty on my head.

The Dark Guard grabbed my wrists and pulled himself away from the tree, pressing his stomach against the tip of my sword. I felt the tender flesh yield to the sharp blade as he slid himself further up the Retaliator until the hilt rested against his abdomen. He collapsed, his head resting against my shoulder as he died. I pushed him off, cursing as his body crumpled to the ground.

"What were you thinking about?" Kellen toed the limp body, turning the guard's head with his foot for a better look at the only exposed part of the face in the mask- the eyes.

"Before he went all Ronin and killed himself? I don't know, about what killing them to keep the king from hearing your lies would mean."

"Quinlan is, or should I say 'was', very adept at reading minds."

"How do you know that?" I asked, unsure if I wanted to know the answer.

"Because he was my brother. Well, half-brother. An unfortunate indiscretion on my father's part with a half-blood Unseelie. He tried to correct the mistake, you see, too bad young Quinlan here survived. A black mark on an otherwise infallible royal house. Back to you, daughter of Arawn. You find yourself in quite a conundrum, Maurin. Ill fated since birth, what a shame for such a beautiful creature to live her life this way. It's as if there is no other course for you half-bloods. Take the queen's offer."

Dre took hold of the only Unseelie who remained conscious so that Conry could join Aidan at my back. "I must respectfully decline."

Aidan leaned in, whispering advice to take the queen's help. We weren't in a position to refuse any longer. Each warrior felt the death of another. The Dark Guard would come to claim their dead and wounded - to claim me. We were tired, barely healed from our last run-in with the guard and taking out the blood coven, basically chasing our tails with no real leads on Mason or my father. A little help would have been nice. His logic made sense, sound advice, but I knew we were better off on our own. I clasped the apple branch charm hanging from my neck and prayed for strength, for clarity to see the offer of help from the Seelie for what it really was. Servitude. There are always strings attached when dealing with the fae, whether you can see them or not.

"We'll be watching, Maurin, as we always have." Kellen reached for me, slipping a hand behind my head and jerking me toward him with a quickness I didn't know he possessed. "In the end, you'll beg for her help. Perhaps my queen will be merciful enough to give it to you." Kellen disappeared, gone as quickly as he'd come. Leaving us to clean up the mess we started with the Unseelie guards.

"What do you want to do with him, er, I think she's a her,actually." Dre jostled the guard causing her hood to slip back.

A shimmering black braid tumbled free contrasting her pale skin. Anger flushed her skin, her nostrils flaring slightly with each deep breath she took struggling against Dre's hold. She took in the sight of her fallen brethren and the sword in my hand, lashing out when she realized what it was. She screamed that the relic belonged to the Court of Shadows, that the fallen Angel had no right to give it to a traitorous half-blood. I could only assume Quinlan's halfblooded nature had been over looked when he agreed to serve the King. Neutrality was an underappreciated trait with the fae.

"Drain her. It'll buy us some time." We needed every second we could get. Her hatred for me was evident in the look in her eyes, each vow to kill me uttered with a conviction that had me more than a little concerned.

Aidan moved in, his eyes locked with mine as he drank the fae to unconsciousness while Dre held her. I could count on one hand the number of times I'd seen Aidan feed from someone other than me. The last time sealed the end of our relationship. That didn't stop the little pang of jealousy or the ghostly sensation of his lips on my neck as he suckled her jugular while I watched. It was a familiar scene, one that stirred up painful memories softened with time and my love for Mason. Just the thought of him was enough to pull me out of Aidan's trance. I broke eye contact, suddenly uncomfortable with the way he looked at me. Aidan wanted something I couldn't give him.More than my blood, he wanted my heart, and I'd already given it to someone else.

Dre pulled in a deep breath through his nose, catching the scent of fae in my blood. Our blood, especially mine because of the magic mixed in, was not only intoxicating, it was addictive if consumed in large quantities or even small amounts over a long period of time. If I wasn't careful, I would end up being the jelly in a vampire sandwich. It was the reason my father convinced Aidan to break things off, in a way that would convince me never to take him back. All of my father's meddling was forgotten thanks to Mason and completely forgiven the moment he disappeared. I refused to believe I'd never have the chance to tell him so. The charm on my necklace warmed, the heat intensifying the more I thought about my father.

I whistled for Conry, missing the familiar jingle of the collar and tags I'd gotten him when he ran to me. I planned on buying him a new studded leather one as soon as possible. "Let's go. I have an idea."

I kept a hand on Conry, more for comfort than the need to touch him when we jumped, while the vampires each clamped a hand on my shoulder. I kept them in the dark, refusing to answer a single question about our destination, until we arrived in front of the Salem witch house. Something had been scratching at the back of my mind since I saw Mahalia's athame back at the blood coven's house, a way to find my father. I mentally kicked myself for not thinking of it sooner.

It felt like a lifetime ago. I considered Mahalia a friend once. We'd faced a triad of goddesses together, joined forces to take down a demon army and in the midst of all that, she called my father for help when it seemed like we weren't going to win. She'd summoned him like he was a demon.

If she could do it, so could Amalie. She contained more power within her than the rest of the coven combined. It sucked that she hadn't come into her power until last year. Amalie had been stunted by the fear of an old crone unwilling to hand over control to a younger witch, even if it was for the benefit of the coven.

Intimidated by her raw capabilities, Mahalia held her back. She never allowed her to study anything other than healing magic so Amalie could never rise to power. If she continued on that path, Amalie could have healed any ailment or injury a person could have, maybe even cancer - knowing her she probably already could. She should have been groomed to take over the coven instead of Oberon. If she had, they wouldn't be leaderless. Even now she denied that Mahalia purposely kept her from her true path. After a lifetime in the woman's care, she was unable to fully understand the depth of Mahalia's ruthlessness.

We stepped out onto the street in front of the coven's headquarters without so much as a pebble crunching beneath our feet, each step soft and silent. After months working together we knew each other's strengths and weaknesses in a fight, knew the best way to watch each other's backs. We fell into familiar positions, moving in a diamond formation. Conry led the pack, Aidan on the right, me on the left and Dre bringing up the rear. There were less than forty paces from where I brought us through the veil to the front door of the coven.

We left four of the Dark Guard lying in a field outside of Danvers. There were at least four more unaccounted for this side of Faerie. Surely they felt the death of Quinlan by now. They were close, I felt their breath on the back of my neck. This had to work, my father had to appear, or we'd be faced with the remaining warriors - most likely at sunrise when I'd be alone.

14

We fanned out in front of the small front porch. I hadn't been here since the night I'd learned of Oberon and Mahalia's betrayal. I remembered the grief I'd felt when I thought Oberon was dead and the anger when I realized he was alive. Shortly after that, Mahalia tried to kill me by banishing me with an Afrit - one of the deadliest of the djinn cast of demons. My father saved me after I slayed the demon, showed me the way out of the plane I'd been banished to. The hate-fueled fire of anger raged, flaring higher with each heartbeat, with each memory, each minute that passed knowing Mahalia was somehow involved in the disappearance of my father and Mason. I'd find them, whatever the cost.

The worn, plastic doorbell glowed a soft orange in the darkness, encouraging visitors to press it and announce their presence. In the face of what lied ahead, I welcomed the normalcy, hitting the button despite tripping a ward when we crossed the yard. The door slowly creaked open on its own, the house welcomed us, which was just as important as being welcomed by the coven. I pushed the door the rest of the way open and stepped inside. My team followed me in just before the house closed the door. No one came to greet us, so I continued into the sunken living room. I felt the magic of the house press against us, seeking out the true purpose of our visit. Satisfied, the pulse slowed and the magic withdrew. Halfway there, I thought. Now I just needed to convince Amalie to help me conjure my father, even if it went against Oberon's wishes.

As if summoned by my thoughts, Amalie descended the two steps into the living room and sat down on the couch. I knew the house told her of our arrival, of our need for help. She connected with the magic here on a level no one expected. A lot changed in the time and distance I'd put between our friendship. I'd been making an effort to mend fences, obviously not enough.

"I stopped by the station, where's Mason?" Amalie's expression said she genuinely didn't know the answer. I had a feeling she could have pulled the information from my mind if she wanted to. Out of respect for our friendship she chose not to.

"I don't know. My father's missing too, I'm not sure what remains of the Wild Hunt. That's why we're here. I need your help, Amalie."

She smiled at the formality of me asking for help. "So we've moved way beyond someone just wanting to kill you. And in just two days. That's a record, even for you. You know I'll help you. Whatever it is."

"There's something you should know first. Mahalia's back."

Amalie went rigid at the mention of the former high priestess's name. "That's not possible. She's been imprisoned in the Court of Light since her trial."

"Look, it's a really long story, but we went after a blood coven tonight..."

"Another one?" She gasped.

"Yeah, they took Conry, tried to turn him into some sort of flesh eater. Anyway, Mahalia was there. We found her athame on an altar room in the basement." My guardian's upper lip curled back exposing his sharp canines, a fierce growl rumbling out of him at the mention of the altar.

"You saw a blade, it looked like hers. That's all." Fear slipped behind her eyes, knowing she might have to face the woman who'd basically bound her magic as a child.

"Kellen confirmed it."

She closed her eyes, taking a deep breath to physically absorb the truth of my words. "Blood covens, I can't believe she's behind them. I never knew she had such darkness inside her."

I crooked a brow. "I did."

"No, you don't understand." She pointed to Aidan and Dre. "People used to think that vampires were dark, evil creatures because they need the blood, the life force of another to live. They don't have to kill. Once the norms realized that, they were pretty much accepted. Now, blood magic? There's a reason it's forbidden, even by the Others. It requires a sacrifice. The harder the spell, the larger the kill. She ran this coven forever. She served the Council even longer. It's hard to imagine the woman I knew is capable of this."

"The same woman who put a cork in your magic? The same woman who put me in a circle with a demon, sent me to another plane in Other World with the hopes that the Afrit or the trip would kill me?"

"I know, Maurin, I'm sorry. I'm trying to understand all this. It's just hard to undo a lifetime of programming."

"It gets worse."

"Worse than realizing the woman you idolized plotted your magical destruction and pissed on the religion you've devoted your life to?"

"We think she's using wild magic somehow. Like she figured out a way to sprinkle a little fae in her spells. We think the Unseelie are helping her or she's helping them."

"Yup, that's definitely worse. We have to tell Oberon. He's the closest thing we have to a unified leader right now."

"It should be you."

"No, it shouldn't. I'm not strong enough to bring all the covens together. Oberon can do that if the Council will ever allow it. This coven is where I belong. So tell me what spell you came here for."

"I don't know the name, or if it's communal, or if Mahalia just made it up as she went." I let out a frustrated breath.

"Well of course you don't. You don't take after your mother's side at all. Damn Faerie genes are way too dominant. Just tell me what it does."

"I'll take that as a compliment, seeing as how witches have caused me nothing but trouble since the day I was born. Look who my mother gave me to. Present company excluded of course." I gave her a little wink and brought the conversation back around to the magic I needed Amalie to work for me. "Mahalia summoned my father with it the night we killed the triad."

"I hate to be the bearer of bad news. It's more than likely Mahalia wove an old prayer into a new spell. Maybe if I knew...." Amalie trailed off, lost in her thoughts, an idea forming in her powerful mind.

I snapped my fingers to get her attention. "Maybe if you knew what? Amalie, if you knew what?"

"We're going to need Oberon's help. Come on." Amalie headed toward the office in the back of the house off the kitchen.

"I was kind of hoping to keep him out of this." I called after her.

"If you want to find your father, we're going to need to dig through some of his old prayer books. He's a druid, Maurin. If anyone knows where to find the original prayer Mahalia used, it'll be him."

"Amalie, is there any way you could procure the book without tipping Oberon off?" Aidan swooped in, draping an arm over her shoulder and steering her back to me.

"I'm serious Amalie, the less people that know about this the better." There were too many people still pledging allegiance to the old priestess. Oberon broke ties after the trial. If he knew about her involvement, he'd be obligated to warn the coven. The last thing we needed was more people enlisting with Mahalia.

"I have to tell him, Maurin." Amalie refused to budge.

Dre broke his silence, echoing my thoughts. "She's running with the Dark Guard and a blood coven. We don't need any more witches going over to the dark side."

"Damn it, Maurin, why is the shit you're in always neck deep? How the hell am I supposed to get the prayer books out of Oberon's office? He practically sleeps in there."

"What about the necromancer?" Dre asked.

"What about her?" It took a second for Amalie to catch on. "Gross Dre."

Once I stopped laughing, I reminded him that we didn't have time to wait for Graive and Oberon to get their freak on. "If I knew how to craft the spell, I wouldn't be dragging you into this mess."

With a snap of her fingers, Amalie took off, ordering us to stay put. She returned a few minutes later with three dusty, old tombs in her arms. "I told him I was helping you with some research since you wanted to know more about where your family came from. Your dad's pretty tight lipped when it comes to your mother. So you asked me to help you trace your lineage."

"And he went for it?" It was too easy. I expected Oberon to jump out and yell "a-ha". "I mean, it's us. He wasn't the least bit suspicious?"

"He handed them right over, said it was good you were finally taking an interest in your history."

"You're absolutely sure he couldn't tell you were lying?" He was head of the coven, he should be able to smell bullshit.

"He's got no reason to suspect me of anything. You, on the other hand, he'd bespell you to tell the truth for sure. Come on, we can't work on this here."

I felt more than a little offended Oberon would suspect me of lying. I wasn't the one living a lie every day we had been together. And then I remembered I'd basically asked Amalie to snatch Oberon's books and to keep a major secret by not telling him about Mahalia. So I guess I deserved a truth spell after all. I left my indignation inside when I followed Amalie out of the house with two vampires and my dog behind me.

We stood in the front yard, everyone looking to me for our destination. The only problem was I didn't have a clue where to go to cast the spell.

"Let's just go back to your apartment."

Everyone who'd been in my apartment recently knew that was a terrible idea. "Um yeah, that's not going to work. There's a dead guy in my living room."

Amalie rolled her eyes. "What about..."

"Trashed and unsecured." I answered before she could suggest Mason's place.

"Come on. I can't believe we're going to do this here. We're going to get caught. And then I'm going to have to explain to Oberon why I'm trying to summon your dad at my kitchen table. I'll be stuck doing all the remedial spells to make charms for the store." Amalie stormed off to the one bedroom apartment she lived in over the garage on the neighboring property. The coven owned the adjoining lots, renting them to different members over the years. Amalie had lived here since Mahalia's trial. I'd yet to see the inside of it.

We followed her up the metal staircase that had been added well over twenty years ago and remained rust free thanks to the coven's magic. One bedroom may have been an overstatement since there were no walls in the whole place, except for the bathroom. Each area flowed freely into the next, the kitchen into living room, the living room into the bedroom. The decor represented every aspect of Amalie's personality. Whimsical netting with little butterflies pinned onto it hung from the ceiling above her bed, bold colored pillows and a throw splashed against a black futon. Prints from Warhol, Degas and Escher fought for space on her walls with tags from local graffiti artists and framed vintage album covers. You felt instantly at home, even while your senses were assaulted by everything around you.

Conry nestled at my feet as the four of us settled around Amalie's fifties style kitchen table. She placed a book in front of each of us with specific instructions to look for anything that mentioned Arawn or Lord of Other World, even the Cwnn Anfwnn. With a snap of her fingers, the percolating coffee pot on her stove fired up and two bags of blood moved from the fridge to the microwave. Samantha from that show *Bewitched* couldn't have been a better hostess than our Amalie.

Comforted by the feel of a warm mug filled with coffee in my hands, I scoured page after page for even one mention of my father, turning up nothing by the time I'd reached the end of my book. In true vampire fashion, Aidan and Dre finished their assigned reading before I did, both coming up empty as well. Amalie scanned the last pages of her book while I drank the last of the coffee. She slammed the cover shut, muffling the sound of a knock at the door. When the second knock sounded, she jumped out of her chair and opened the door with all of the enthusiasm of a little girl walking toward an inevitable punishment.

Oberon stood on the platform outside the door, arms crossed over his chest, Graive leaned against the railing behind him. They both looked the part of scolding parents, except Amalie was an adult and not their kid. Still I knew we were caught so I scrambled to come up with an explanation that wasn't lying and wasn't the complete truth either - even a half-blood should be able to manage that fae trick.

I knew I'd been spelled the minute I opened my mouth and the whole sordid story spilled out from the assassination attempts and the death spell that jumped from person to person, to the blood covens Mahalia was leading from her prison in Faerie, to her escape and involvement with the Unseelie. As pissed as I was about the truth spell, the shock on Oberon and Graive's face kept me from saying anything about it. Amalie told them to come in off the porch and waved her hand sending two chairs sliding over to the table. She'd definitely been working on her kinetic energy since the last time I saw her.

We spent the next hour going over everything again in greater detail. My leg tapped under the table, my impatience started to get the better of me. I'd hoped to have the spell cast by now, to have my father here and be working on a plan to find Mason. Too much time went by without word from his captors. No ransom, no threats for his death if I didn't comply with their requests. I refused to believe he was already dead. I would know, I would feel it, if the single most important person in my life ceased to exist. This was the longest I'd sat down since this whole mess started. My leg tapped faster as my thoughts ran away from me. We needed to pick up the pace, a little less conversation a little more action. Aidan reached under the table, laying a heavy hand on my knee, holding it still. He leaned in, whispering in my ear that we were almost ready.

Oberon agreed to help Amalie perform the spell. Any sentimental feelings he held onto for Mahalia vanished when he learned she was behind the blood covens. He stood, pulling a small prayer book from his back pocket. He held out a hand for Amalie. She reached across the table, her chair scooting across the old linoleum, as she got to her feet. Oberon set the palm-sized book in the center of the table. The smooth leather cover flipped open, the frail pages turning rapidly before coming to an abrupt stop. The spine stretched until the stitching threatened to pop. With hands clasped across the table, the two witches began a prayer to the Lord of the Other World. Oberon led the prayer, changing the pace and order of the words as they went. Amalie followed, their voices getting louder with each repetition of the prayer turned spell.

Arawn Lord of Annwfn, I call to thee

Master of the Cwnn Annwfn, I call to thee

Set your hunters free

Conry shifted his weight from paw to paw, the words igniting some primal need to run down prey. Magic charged the air, tiny tendrils of electricity flicked across my skin seconds before the room shifted. The floor shook, cabinet doors swung open, dishes crashed to the floor. The power grew, pressing against the walls until glass shattered from the few windows in the small apartment. The current of power settled, the spell suddenly neutralized. A breeze blew in from the broken windows, stirring the remnants of the spell until all that remained was the scent of ozone, that summer thunderstorm smell.

Everyone in the room stood still, baffled by the failure. The magic should have worked, if not my father then someone from the hunt should have appeared. Things looked worse than I thought if the hunters and hounds refused the call. Conry whined and pawed at the spot where I stared in disbelief. Even my guardian understood what it meant for us that no one came. I opened the front door and told him to go outside. He paused at the threshold, looking back to make sure it was okay to leave my side. I knelt down and wrapped my arms around his thick neck, his muzzle resting on my shoulder. He licked my neck a few times while I rubbed his back and whispered in his ear to run. Words have power, more so when a witch speaks them. I knew Amalie and Oberon did everything right, I could feel the reaction in Conry. He overflowed with energy, bounding down the metal staircase into the yard to burn some of it off.

"I don't understand what went wrong." Unfamiliar with failure, Amalie sank down on the floor next to me, dropping her head into the spot where Conry's was.

"From the looks of that dog, I'd say the spell was a success." Graive pulled her hair back in a low ponytail and grabbed a broom from the tiny hall closet. She started cleaning up the magical aftermath while the rest of us tried to figure out what to do next.

Aidan and Dre suggested refining the spell which Oberon vehemently refused. They'd expended far too much energy the first time. Of course, the vampires couldn't understand how two dozen words could be that draining. Amalie just rolled her eyes and let out a sigh of exasperation. For all their time together, working alongside each other under the Council's guidance, they didn't really understand how the other worked. They learned as much as they needed to in order to function together, nothing more. To say it complicated things was an understatement.

Conry barked uncontrollably, sounding off the alarm that something was wrong outside. The wards around the property hadn't been broken, not even when the Afrit came looking for me in the main house. I'd be lying if I said I didn't wonder if Mahalia took them down to let the demon in. I never had a chance to ask her how long she plotted against me before they whisked her away to prison.

Graive crept to the window, peeking out through what remained of the glass. "Four men across the street. Do you think it's the Hunt? Maybe the spell worked after all."

"It's not the Hunt." I didn't need to look outside to know who was waiting on the other side of the wards. "It's more of the Dark Guard."

"How do you know that, you haven't even looked?"

"Because that's how my fucking day has been going so far, Graive."

"So what do we do now, Maurin?" Amalie sounded like she was ready for a fight. I needed to calm her down. The coven couldn't get any deeper in this than they already were.

"We aren't doing anything. I'm going to talk outside."

"The wards are holding, don't go out there. Two witches, two vampires and a necro, we can come up with something." Aidan blocked the door.

"You know as well as I do that the wards are only holding because they haven't tried to take them down." I went to him, resting a hand on his cheek. He turned his face until his lips rested against my palm, placing the softest of kisses in the cup of my hand. "A necro isn't going to be much help here. It's not like we have a supply of corpses for her to raise. No offense, Graive." She waived my comment off, knowing full well she didn't have anything to work with against the Dark Guard. "Dawn isn't far off. You and Dre need to head to Risqué, meet up with the rest of the team. You'll be secure there during the day."

"We can help, we'll call in the rest of the coven. Maurin, you can't do this alone." Amalie looked to Oberon expecting to see him in solidarity with her, with me. Her eyes brimmed with tears when he looked away and dropped his head.

"We can't call the rest of the coven, Amalie." He knew the risks as well as I did. If the Dark Guard was in fact working with Mahalia, any remaining loyalists would defect the minute they found out. Oberon needed time to clean up the coven himself, make sure no one was helping her from inside and reveal her involvement in the blood covens before she could lure them away and taint them with dark magic.

"It's going to be fine. I've got Conry and I've got the Retaliator. Plus the necklace. Kellen said it grants the wearer safe passage." Confidence rang from my voice despite being smacked in the face with disadvantage after disadvantage. My friends were incredibly loyal and powerful, but each had a weakness the Dark Guard could exploit. "I'm just going to talk with them. If they were looking for a fight, they'd have dropped the wards already. If they make a move, Conry and I will jump out of here."

"Parlay? Seriously, that's your plan?"

"They're fae not pirates, Dre. You've been watching Pirates of the Caribbean again, haven't you?" I gave him a little wink, trying to lighten the heavy mood in the room.

"Now is not the time for bad jokes, Maurin. You said it yourself, they'll see you stand trial or dead for what we did in Danvers. Aidan and I drained three guardsmen and a fourth died by your sword."

Amalie gasped when she heard what Dre said. "Maurin, you didn't? They'll kill you for that."

"It's not as bad as it sounds." I gave Dre a stern look, silently telling him to shut up. It probably was as bad as it sounded. Unfortunately we were out of options. I glanced around the room at the faces, the friends gathered to help me and was hit with a moment of clarity. Something was rotten in Faerie and I wound up stuck in the middle of it.

"Look, I can't risk you two getting burned to a crisp if they whisk us away to Faerie and it just happens to be high noon when we arrive and I can't risk the coven falling into Mahalia's hands. Which I'm afraid is a very real possibility and probably why they're not dropping the wards, because of some agreement with Mahalia. If you continue to harbor the enemy, they may change their minds. We've tried running, we've tried to force information out of them, which in hindsight was way too easy to do or would have been if Kellen hadn't shown up. And why did he show up, huh? Because I for one seriously doubt it was to help us. We even tried magic and none of that worked. We're no closer to finding Mason or my father. We're being played."

Never a fan of long good byes, I headed out to join Conry in the yard and face off with a few more members of the Dark Guard.

15

I stood at the edge of the yard, concealed from the waist down by the boxwood hedge. Conry growled a warning to the Guard over the bushes, hackles raised at the potential threat. If I wanted to hear what the Unseelie had to say, my guardian and I needed to keep our cool. My right hand instinctively ran along the top of his head and down his back, trying to keep him calm while the Retaliator remained hidden in my left.

Neither side said anything. Seconds ticked painfully by in an awkward silence. The eyes watching from the apartment above burned into my back. The Dark Guard seemed as uncomfortable as me, uncertain if they should make the first move. Often accused of having more balls than brains, I decided to make the first move. I could feel Aidan shaking his head from two stories away, which for some reason only encouraged me more.

"Come here often?" The Guard shared a puzzled expression and Conry huffed at my attempt at humor. Admittedly my comedic timing has been off lately, but it wasn't that bad. Down to business then. "Where's my father and the rest of the Hunt?"

"The king requires your presence at the Court of Shadows." The leader of the Guard stepped forward, his black on black uniform making him nearly invisible in the darkness. Variations in the sheen of the threading caught the moonlight, highlighting the king's crest on the chest of his tunic.

"Look, you all started coming after me first." I counted off on my fingers. "First with London, then the spell, you shot me at Mason's apartment, with iron you know how much that hurts, you gave my dog to a blood coven, kidnapped my father and boyfriend. You drew first blood, all I did was strike back. We could have killed them all, I didn't even kill Quinlan. He did that himself." I may have said too much.

Two of the Guard stepped forward, moving around their leader. From the shared angry glances and aggressive posture it was obvious they weren't here about the incident in Danvers. The leader threw his arms out, the force to hold back his brethren evident in the strain on his face.

"The king requires your presence in the Court of Shadows to discuss other matters. Though I am sure as you might expect these transgressions will be brought before him." A bead of sweat ran down his brow as he ground out the words.

"A meeting with the king, safe passage to and from his court for my guardian and myself?" From my peripheral I saw Amalie and Aidan watching from the window. I knew each word carried easily enough for a vampire across the yard, even still Amalie spun a spell to ensure every syllable hit their ears with perfect clarity. Their fear equally clear when I looked at them.

"The relic hanging from your neck ensures it. Why ask it of us?" The malice in his eyes spoke volumes.

"I would have your word on this matter or you'll be forced to disappoint your king."

"You have our word no harm will come to you while you are in the king's court."

With Conry at my side, I walked the short distance across the street, resisting the urge to shudder when the wards peeled away from my skin. Walking into a ward only alerted the person who set it, walking out of a ward of protection, on the other hand, was like being pushed through a wall of jello. After one last glance over my shoulder and a wave good bye to my friends, the leader of the guard opened the veil and ushered us through.

No sooner did my foot hit the grey fog I got blindsided with a stiff right hand to the temple. My knees threatened to buckle from taking a fist to the head. Somehow, I managed to keep myself upright. When the second and third came in a right-left combination to my mouth and eye I doubled over, my face hitting the leader's back on the way down. Punches in bunches, I'd been practicing similar techniques for working on the inside in a fight, but the fae currently handing me my ass was faster than any sparring partner I'd had to date. After wiping my blood on the leader's tunic, thankfully it was hidden by the dark fabric, I stood back up in time to catch a shot in the solar plexus, knocking the wind out of me. I took a knee and stayed there, holding on to Conry's collar the whole time I was down. He wanted to retaliate, pulling against my hold on the collar. If the Dark Guard wanted to play, we'd play. I'd go into the court looking every bit the victim. It might not gain favor or sympathy from the king. I'd already done enough to incur his wrath. Unleashing my Cwnn Anfwnn and the Retaliator would only make things worse.

"Enough." The leader of the guard roared, throwing the guardsman to the ground.

"You said no harm would come to her in the king's court, Cirian. I haven't broken any oath, we agreed to nothing regarding the trip there."

"You try my patience, Elowyn." The leader, Cirian, hauled me to my feet as I spat blood out of my mouth. It may have been in Elowyn's general direction. I remained firmly planted in front of Cirian for the remainder of the trip.

The grey beneath our feet shifted into a black stone floor. The remaining fog dissipated revealing smooth, obsidian walls, like black mirrors casting our reflection. Conry's white fur stood out, a stark contrast to the darkness that surrounded us. Wrought iron torches protruded from the walls casting soft, orange light along the hallway. Our breath hung in the cold air, tiny ice crystals forming with each exhale. The Court of Shadows was a bitter, desolate place. No signs of comfort or respite, this was a place meant to echo every scream and reflect every torment in its glassy surface.

The hall opened up to a great chamber with massive columns supporting the domed ceiling. The king sat upon a throne of charred bone, awaiting our arrival. Cirian shoved me into the room. The rubber soles of my combat boots skidded across the floor, breaking the silence and drawing the king's attention.

"You've proven yourself to be a formidable adversary. You've thwarted numerous attempts on your life, evaded my Guard, and bested four of them."

"I think someone has been grossly overstating my accomplishments. And I wasn't aware that we were adversaries."

"Perhaps it's time for a different approach." He swung one leather clad leg over the arm of his chair, bobbing a booted foot up and down. The long, fur rimmed cloak fell open exposing his bare chest covered in tattoos very similar to the markings on my spine. He was as handsome as he was half-crazed. "Shall we discuss recent events, perhaps a meeting of the minds? I'll go first. I was shocked to hear news of Quinlan's death, and at the hands of a half-blood in possession of an Unseelie relic. Imagine my dismay." Rough hands pulled at the hair by his temples, mussing the perfectly pleated braid in his raven black hair.

Conry stirred at my side, picking up on my increased tension. Up shit creek without a paddle didn't cover it. I'd fed three of the Guard to vampires and was indirectly responsible for the death of the king's nephew. It looked more and more like Conry and I'd be jumping out of Faerie.

"I didn't kill your nephew."

"Try to justify it as much as you like, he died at your hand. Such a waste. You had so much in common. Caste aside at birth, denied by his father. Half-breed, like you. If you'd only taken the time to get to know him."

"We weren't at group therapy. I thought he had information I needed so I used the sword as a conversation starter. He wasn't in a talking mood. Kellen said..."

"Kellen." Acid all but dripped from the king's mouth when he spoke the Seelie warrior's name. "Did he tell you how he and his mother encouraged his father to rip Quinlan from my sister's womb? Their piety knows no bounds. Liars, murderers, thieves, all of them. That gilded whore sits upon her throne casting judgment when she's the worst of us all. We don't hide what we are beneath a glamour.

"The friend of my enemy is also my enemy. You should have picked your allies more carefully, Maurin. I'd planned an evening of enlightening conversation. After spending some time with you, I can see you require visual aids."

I had no clue what was happening, completely and utterly confused - almost as much as King Ballard seemed to be. The unmistakable sound of bare flesh dragged across glass echoed behind me. I refused to turn around. The king planned this, all of it. His false outrage and lunacy, every moment, every move led up to this.

A servant dressed in a billowing ombre gown in shades of silver and grey escorted two men into the hall. The fae wore garb similar to a medieval huntsman made from worn, dark brown leather. Chains rattled and clanked with each tug as they pulled the prisoners behind them. It was a familiar sound, stirring up memories of the night Mahalia was brought before the Council. I held the king's gaze, unwilling to give him the reaction he wanted.

"I'm pleased to see you know even a half-blood is above a werewolf. My spies told me these dogs meant something to you." Ballard jumped off his throne, landing in front of them. "String them up." His hand swung up in an exaggerated gesture toward the ceiling.

The two hunters grabbed a large hook, snaring the chain. Metal teeth clicked together, gears wound, powering a machine hidden somewhere behind the walls. Slowly, Cash and Nolak inched forward, their beaten bodies trapped in their human form thanks to the silver pins driven into their flesh. Conry scratched at the floor as they passed, while I did my best to remain calm as my friends were suspended from the ceiling. Cash and Nolak handled the pain better than I would have, never uttering a sound. With the first wrist pop, I couldn't hold my tongue any longer.

"What do you want from me?" My cries bounced off the bare walls, echoing back. Ballard just smiled and motioned for one of his men to hoist the alpha and his second higher. "Stop, stop! Just tell me what you want!"

I came here expecting answers, information to help me find my father and Mason. I knew it was risk, one I was willing to take even if everything Kellen said proved to be true. I hadn't seen this coming, however. Ballard threw down the ace up his sleeve and there was no way I could beat him. All I could do was find out what he wanted. I prayed it was something I could give him.

The king kicked a switch in the floor I hadn't seen before, sending Cash and Nolak down in a rush. Their bodies bounced with the impact before skin slicked with sweat and blood suctioned to the tile. Neither moved nor so much as whimpered. Fear they are were dead coursed through my veins. Ballard knew exactly how to break me. Torture me, you may get some satisfying tears or screams of pain. I'd been through it before and lived to tell the tale. But this? He had me right where he wanted me. He knew I wouldn't stand by and let my friends die, not if there was something I could do about it. And Ballard seemed to think there was. Something other than fighting him because the king was undefeated. He was as ruthless and deadly as his Seelie counterpart.

"I'll help you, just let them go. Whatever it is, I'll help you." Aidan would likely kill me for getting myself into this mess. Ballard left me no choice. My necklace ensured my safe return and I had the word of the Dark Guard I wouldn't be harmed. The Salem pack would not be destroyed because of me. I tried to do things differently, to do things according to plan, and I still ended up here.

I ran to Cash and Nolak, hovering over them searching for signs of life. Conry settled in beside them, nudging their limp bodies with his muzzle. I managed to pry three silver stakes free from Cash before I felt the crack of a whip across my back. Blood instantly soaked my shirt, my skin torn as easily as the cotton fabric. I grabbed a fistful of pins more from both Nolak and Cash, they needed to shift in order to heal the damage.

Hard leather ripped across my back again, bringing me to my knees. A couple of the needles I dropped on the floor drove up into my palm when I slammed my hands down on the floor to keep from falling over. Conry rushed the king, lunging for his throat. With a snap of his fingers, Ballard dropped my guardian to the floor. Conry writhed in pain before submitting to the king's will.

"Did you know that the Cwnn Anfwnn once belonged to the Unseelie court?" Ballard walked around the limp body of my dog, a disgusted look on his face as he nudged Conry's belly. "I can tell by the look on your face that he didn't bother with history lessons. Your father and everything in Other World once belonged to the Court of Shadows. It seems that even after he successfully seceded from my predecessor he forgot one small detail. The source of creation still holds power over the thing it created.

"As for you, I think I quite like the sight of you on your knees. For so many reasons." Ballard sexually assaulted me with his eyes. "Denounce the Court of Light and your friends will walk out of here. Refuse the queen's request and I'll consider allowing you to join them. Or keep you for my concubine. I have become rather bored with my harem." The tips of King Ballard's boots stopped at the small pool of blood forming under my palms.

"What request? She didn't ask for anything." He stepped forward, the ball of his foot coming down on my hand, grinding the sole of his shoe against my knuckles. "She offered to help me find Mason and my dad, that's all."

"Your majesty," Cirian paused. "She wears the branch. No harm is to come to her."

"I am well aware of the charm that hangs from her neck and what it means. And the foolish promise you made. Never speak for your king." Ballard rushed the head of his guard, slicing a blade from the corner of Cirian's mouth to mid cheek. The iron blade would ensure slow healing and a scar as a physical reminder of his insolence. "It was in her mother's possession at one point. The relic seems drawn to her bloodline. I should like to spill some more and study its properties, see what makes you so desirable. Perhaps later in my private chambers. The charm grants safe passage. Of course, there isn't a hard fast rule as to when that is supposed to happen, only that I release you." Ballard snapped his fingers, gesturing for someone to be brought in the room.

My heart beat wildly with the ridiculous hope that either one of the men I'd been searching for would walk through the doorway, only to be crushed again when another fae, dressed in a more elaborate version of the hunters' clothing came in. The woodsman bent over the wolves, his open hands hovered above them, palm down. Powered ebbed and flowed, building and building until it pulled out, rushing back in like a tsunami. All of that energy focused on Cash and Nolak, finally breaking the men where everyone else failed.

Grunts of pain, followed by howls, ricocheted around the room. Bones cracked, shifted, as their bodies morphed from man to beast. Fur sprouted, claws scratched the floor. Normal canines elongated, sharpened into deadly weapons used to rend flesh from bone. The only remnants of their humanity remained in the eyes, every emotion conveyed in the dark orbs, like pain. The forced shift looked horrific. Cash and Nolak's sides heaved with each heavy pant, their tongues lolled out of the side of their muzzles as they fought to catch their breath.

I'd heard stories of fae gifted with the ability to control animals. Some controlled the elements, manipulating the rain, wind and sun. Others controlled the earth, plants and minerals. Rarer, were the fae who could control something with free will. This woodsman, one of the few directly connected to the life of every creature, used that gift to cause pain. The fae ripped the beast out of the man, flipping them inside out. Wild magic overrode the pack's, none of the energy instinctive to the wolves for dulling the pain of a shift surfaced.

Every terrible moment of joints popping, bones morphing, tendons and muscles tearing and reconnecting, felt by my friends and visible as they lay on the floor exhausted. With more to heal thanks to the excruciating transformation, Cash and Nolak needed to stay in their animal form longer. My hand instinctively reached for them, fingertips extended in an effort to at least graze their coats, desperate to console them, only to come up short.

"How touching. You could have prevented this, spared their pain. Four little words and they are free to go."

"This is crazy. I have no agreement with the queen."

"Do you not know how to count? That's more than four words. Ballard snatched me up off the floor by my hair, backing me against the cold obsidian wall. He yanked my head back, exposing my neck. He pressed his nose against the base of my neck, sniffing his way up to the back of my ear. "Your scent, your fear is intoxicating. It's what drew me to your mother. You remind me so much of her, like Helen of Troy her face was the catalyst for war. The rife between friends, separating fae from fae." He pressed his entire body against mine, forcing the air from my lungs. "Will you be the reason for war between the courts again?"

"I don't have an agreement with the queen." I struggled to say each word, his full weight crushing my ribs and diaphragm. Ballard backed away, leaving me to slide down the wall.

"You know, I think I actually believe you. Perhaps we can strike a bargain after all."

"I'm listening." I didn't bother to get up. I could hear the offer just fine from the floor.

Arawn rarely spoke of my mother, apart from the story of how I ended up with the Kincaides, or the occasional mention of her power when he tried to teach me something. The story of how my mother fractured Faerie or how Conry once belonged to the king never came up. My father scolded me on more than one occasion about not taking enough interest in my heritage, the Others or Other World, but it seemed like he only wanted me to learn what he deemed important. My mother spent time in the court with the king - this was information that I could have used. I felt ill equipped for the negotiations.

Ballard held the advantage. He knew more than I did and information is a dangerous weapon - especially when an arrangement with the king was my only ticket out of there. If I pushed, I could use the charm and walk out of there. Odds were, I'd be walking out alone. I wouldn't leave without Conry, Cash or Nolak so I did the only thing I could. Waited and listened to the king's offer.

"Tianna, my lovely wife, wants to unite the courts. And by that I mean eradicate the Unseelie. Take us back to the time when there was no Court of Shadows, no creatures of the dark.

She's convinced herself that the glittering bastards flitting around her court are better than my children. I assure you that is not the case. True, there are some forced to live off of others, your vampire friends, for example, once belonged to the darkness. Before they walked amongst the humans they served the Court of Shadows. The ancestors of your wolves once graced these halls as well. Are they so terrible?

"Don't answer that. It was a rhetorical question. Of course they aren't. Her beautiful little Faeries feed off of humanity in other ways, no less tainted than us. Yet they wish to destroy us. And she means to use you to do it."

"I told you, I didn't agree to anything. Especially not help her destroy the dark court. Not that I even could. One half-blood against the entire Court of Shadows? Impossible."

"I told myself the same thing, yet here we are. Swear allegiance to the dark court. Align yourself with me and stand against the queen."

"The price of our freedom is awfully high,Your Highness. The repercussions of this truce are far reaching and long lasting."

"You'd prefer to stay here? I'm flattered."

"Don't be. I didn't say that I wouldn't do it, just that you need to sweeten the pot. I want Mahalia. You set her free, tainted her magic. She's running loose, setting up blood covens. Behind bars or by my sword, her punishment will be served."

"I let her out?" Ballard's mouth split into a grin, a deep raucous laugh worked its way up from the depth of his belly, shaking his body. "Who told you that? Kellen? Tianna?"

"Fae can't lie."

"Best myth we ever started in my opinion. We certainly can, omitting, evading, eluding it's all the same as lying. I would have thought a woman in your line of work would be better at sniffing out falsehoods. You've always relied on your gifts haven't you? Never quite able to stand on your own two feet."

"I'm not through listing my terms." I filled my voice with false bravado, it wasn't fooling anyone.

"My, my, my. Getting emboldened again aren't we? Shall I remind you of your place in my court, Maurin daughter of Arawn?"

"No need. I'm almost done. Three things. Mahalia, my father and Mason. The agreement is between you and me, in no way does it bind Arawn to you. I walk out of here with my friends and family and you have a deal."

"Now whose price is too high? I can't give you what I don't have. Your friends here tonight and you in exchange for your help with the little problem with my wife."

It was my turn to laugh. I pushed myself up of the floor, using the wall for support. "The queen is more than a little problem. Neither of you can say where Mason or my father are. I know one of you is responsible for their disappearance. My allegiance remains where my heart resides: with the Wild Hunt and my father."

"That's a shame, a terrible mistake. I'll give you the opportunity to change your mind. For their sake." Ballard gestured to Conry, Cash and Nolak.

I had a plan, well not a plan so much as a hope. What if I could alter the charm? If I invoked it, mixed it with enough of my magic I could jump the four of us out. It was a long shot and if it didn't play out, the king would dole out a punishment far worse than I'd seen so far. It was a risk I had to take. I grasped the charm, filled my mind with new purpose, with the will and intent to get out of the dark court. All four of us.

"Naughty, naughty girl. I know what you're up to. You will not leave here with those dogs. Swear loyalty to me!"

"No. I gave my terms, you gave yours. We didn't agree. Negotiations have ended. So has the torture."

The charm blazed to life, searing my skin again. Power rippled through me, wild magic mixing with something else, something hidden and untouched. A part of me I didn't know existed roared up from the depths of my soul, radiating out to surround my friends. It continued to pour out of me, unbridled and beyond my control. Still weak from the stress and physical punishment during my stay in the dark court, my body gave out. The floor seemed miles away, the fall in slow motion with King Ballard's screams echoing in my ears.

16

I woke up later in my apartment. My somewhat-clean-and-corpse-free apartment. Soft hues of pinks, oranges and purples washed the sky as day embraced the coming night outside my window. It was a beautiful sunset. One worthy of appreciation despite the chaos that ruled my life. The familiar and comforting weight of Conry beside me in bed gave me solace, a sense of peace I hadn't felt in a long time. I couldn't recall how many days had passed since the whole thing started, I'd probably have to start counting from the day of my birth because this trouble was older than a few days.

If I stayed cuddled up in bed with my guardian, relishing the quiet that managed to find my room despite everything, I could almost pretend nothing happened. The freshly brewed coffee wafting its way down the hall made by none other than Mason, fixed just the way I like it, in my Day of the Dead mug. If I stayed there under the covers, he'd come through the bedroom door, his jeans hung low on his hips accentuating those perfect abs and V dipping just below the waistband, pausing for effect before bringing me my first coffee fix. He'd hand me the mug, slide in under the blankets beside me and I'd curl up against him while I savored the smell and taste of the dark roast, his hand tracing lazy patterns on my arm.

No amount of wishing or dreaming would make that happen. The rib cage, once a container for the wild beast that was my heart felt empty, hollow. Nothing beat ferociously against it, rattling the bars in an effort to break free. My thoughts and mood turned dark with nightfall. The two single most important men in my life were still some where beyond my reach, their lives in peril, and so far I failed them. I tried to fight off the wave of disappointment, self-doubt and hatred.

I failed at that too.

With the beautiful delusion that Mason would walk into my room any second long gone, I forced myself to get out of bed. Defeat slowed my steps. I sluggishly shuffled my way to the kitchen in the dark. Friends sat around my kitchen table like a campfire, huddling over their cups to ward off the chill in the air. With hushed voices they asked questions and exchanged theories about how I managed to get all four of us out of Faerie when the relic was meant for one.

Amalie seemed to think Conry was an extension of me and that dormant magic from my mother's side distorted the purpose of the charm, allowing me to extend it to two more.

Aidan was adamant that fae relics were wild things, with a will of their own, responding to who or what they please. No two people will have the same result using the same relic. Dre felt that as the daughter of Arawn Lord of Other

World and Siobhan, its former owner, it recognized something in me. The power surge Cash and Nolak described was the relic adjusting to me and my request. I stayed in the hallway, listening to them try to make sense of a situation they hadn't even experienced firsthand. The theories became more outlandish so I decided to show my face.

Without saying a word to anyone, I made a beeline to the coffee pot, pouring out the perfect portion to be mixed with sugar and cream. The spoon tinked against the side of the ceramic mug, swirling the ingredients until blended to just the right color and sweetness. I felt the weight of their eyes on me, their words hanging in the air. I took a sip of my coffee, gaining strength from the act of doing something routine, before turning to face them.

"It's pointless trying to figure out how it happened. The relic bent to my will, answered my call. It did what the elders created it to do. For now, that's enough for me. We've got bigger problems than one fae charm." I topped off my cup and sat down at the table.

"We've got more problems than we can handle. We need help, Maurin." Amalie feared going up against Mahalia. The old witch was the last item on my to-do list.

"I've spent more time in Faerie in the last twenty-four hours than I have my entire life and I wouldn't care if I ever stepped foot inside it again. I managed to pick up a few things while I was there."

"You've been gone longer than a day. We thought Kellen snatching you off to the Court of Light was bad. Man, you really had us worried this time." Dre clasped a hand over mine, giving it a reassuring squeeze.

"How long? How long was I at the dark court?" I suspected longer based on how I felt, exhausted even after finally getting some sleep.

"Three days. We sent Cash and Nolak off as soon as you showed up outside my apartment unconscious. They needed pack magic to fully heal and Cash needed to reassure his wolves that their alpha lived. I brought a couple friends here while you were gone, worked a little magic, got the place cleaned up for you. The smell was the worst."

"Thanks Amalie. It's good to be home. I feel like I can finally think for the first time since all of this started."

"And what are you thinking?" Aidan leaned back in his chair, balanced only on the two back legs, analyzing everything I did. Each breath, the tone of my voice, any tell in my expression that would clue him into to what was going on inside my head.

"Two courts, two leaders and I'm stuck somewhere in the middle."

"The king is clearly trying to kill you, the Dark Guard is after you. He set Mahalia free. The queen offers you her help. How are you stuck in the middle? You should accept her help."

"Come on Aidan, think about it for a second. Mahalia's escape was too easy. Not one prison guard saw anything and why didn't they tell us she escaped before? We could have been looking for her all this time. Instead, we've been spinning our wheels going after the blood coven when we could have been after the source."

Aidan whipped out his cell phone, and started texting. His fingers moved across the screen faster than a teen girl's during prom season. I knew the minute he got his answer, from the twitch in his jaw, it wasn't the one he wanted. "Agrona said no one on the Council had been informed of Mahalia's escape."

"Kellen would have us believe otherwise. If I'd thought about it for half a second, I'd have realized, Council or not, if Mahalia was out, Cash would have told me."

"She's got a point, Aidan. It's looking like the queen isn't the ally you hoped she'd be." Dre came around to my way of thinking pretty quickly. "So what's her play?"

"Why set Mahalia free? How is that going to help win you over?" Amalie refilled her coffee mug without getting up. "Not to mention the blood magic, that's not very Seelie-like."

"Light and dark have preconceived notions. I don't think there's much difference between the courts. Ballard mentioned a war, fae against fae, something to do with my mother and then he asked if I was going to be the reason for a second war."

"What the hell is he talking about? What war?" Amalie's finger swirled above her mug, stirring the coffee.

"Well, if I knew where my dad was, I'd ask him. Best I can tell, the queen wants something from me. Something she's willing to do anything to get. She wants me backed in a corner, thinking Ballard and Mahalia are in bed together."

Amalie rubbed her eyes. "Gross, I wonder if there's a spell to erase that image from my mind."

"I don't doubt Ballard has been trying to kill me. The Dark Guard made that pretty clear. I think it was a twisted attempt to stop me from helping his wife."

"Ex-wife." Dre corrected.

"I think it depends on who you ask." My stomach rumbled, reminding me I hadn't eaten in a while. "Can we move this conversation to a place that has food? I'm starving." I scooted my chair back from the table just as someone knocked on the door. "Who the hell could that be?"

"I've got it. I ordered pizza while you were asleep. Dre, hand me my purse please." Amalie paid the delivery man and walked back in to the kitchen with two large pizzas. "I wasn't sure what you'd be in the mood for, so I got one veggie and one linguisa with banana peppers."

"Have I ever told you that I love you?" I grabbed the box holding the ingenious combination of Portuguese sausage, spicy peppers and pizza, downing the first slice in four bites.

Aidan grabbed a bottle of water from the fridge and handed it to me. "Could you come up for air long enough to finish explaining what the hell is going on?"

I took a swig of the water and tossed my crust under the table for Conry. He didn't need to eat food like regular dogs, but had taken a liking to table scraps. My father did not approve of his new eating habits.

"You're just about up to speed. The queen and king both asked me to swear allegiance to their respective crowns in exchange for ridding me of my problems and finding Mason and my dad. Actually, that was the queen's offer. The king's was more like swear it or your friends die and you'll spend eternity in my bedroom." At their horrified expressions, I reassured them I was paraphrasing. "The queen let Mahalia go and she wants me to think the king did it. The king would see me dead before she could trick me into helping her. So whatever it is they think I can do must be pretty fucking huge."

"Where does that leave Mason and your father?" Dre rinsed the glass he'd used to warm his bagged blood in the sink.

"In the cell Mahalia once occupied, of course."

"I just knew you were going to say that. I knew she was going to say that." Amalie looked at Aidan, hoping he'd argue against me and find some flaw in my logic.

"It makes the most sense. You can attract more flies with honey. If that didn't work she'd certainly use venom to get the job done."

I gave Dre a puzzled look. "I'm not sure if I followed that analogy. Though I'd have to agree, she'd have a backup plan. Something I couldn't refuse. Holding my father and

Mason hostage, demanding my cooperation as ransom would definitely qualify."

"So now what? Now that we know, what are we supposed to do?" Amalie's power crackled, building in time with her growing anxiety.

"Let me guess. You want to storm the castle?" Aidan managed to look smug and disapproving. Which of course just irritated the hell out of me.

"No." I crossed my arms over my chest, agitated that he knew me so well.

"We're at a tactical disadvantage. You need to think, plan." Aidan, like all vampires, was all about planning and then planning some more.

After all, when you have eternity, there's no need to rush. You calculated the risks, acceptable casualties and took your time. Years, we're talking decades, centuries if necessary.

I heard a story about a vampire slighted by one of his kin during the dark ages, waiting until long after the industrial revolution to exact his revenge taking out an entire bloodline. So many years passed that none of the undead remembered the offense. The vampire authority convicted him, but he met the sun with a smile on his face. Mason and my father would be dead if I planned my attack on vampire time.

"Do you want to hear my idea or not?" Arms still crossed, I leaned back in my chair, waiting.

"Please, continue." Aidan waved me on with a sarcastic air.

"We accept the queen's offer."

"That's it? We accept her offer?"

"Ease up." Dre clamped a hand on Aidan's shoulder, giving a reassuring squeeze. "Let her finish."

Aidan laughed. "The two of you may have become friends, but I know her better than you. Trust me on this mate, that's as far in the planning process as she got."

"What about the king, Maurin?" Amalie sounded uncertain. She'd taken part in more than one harebrained idea of mine. "He was all 'join the dark side'. I don't think he'll appreciate your walk toward the light."

"I can see by the fact that you worked two movie references in there that you're freaked out by the idea. I need you to stay with me here. We have to keep the king in the dark. No pun intended. Look, both courts have spies. A lot of spies. There's no way we could give the king a heads up without tipping off the queen. I tell the queen that if she gives me my father and Mason I'll help her. I'll use the relic to get us out."

"What if the relic doesn't work? You said it yourself, they can be fickle. What if you get stuck there? How are we supposed to get you out? I've done far too much waiting. I'm dying to see a little action." Dre cracked his knuckles for emphasis.

"When I said 'us', I didn't mean me and Conry. I could use the back up."

"Dying is exactly what you're going to see, Dre, if we go along with this plan. The queen will kill you when she realizes you've tricked her or the king will kill you when he hears you're working with the queen." Aidan wasn't on board, but he wasn't offering any alternatives either. He caught the irritated look I gave him, leaning in close. "I have a dinner to cash in on. I can't do that if you're dead, darling."

I didn't take the bait, jumping up instead and rushing toward the front door. He said 'cash', which reminded me of my friend. It occurred to me that I hadn't checked in on my favorite werewolf since I woke up. I hated to ask for his help again so soon.

"Talk amongst yourselves for a second I need to talk to Cash. Make sure he's okay and let him know what we're planning. He might not be up for it after his visit to the Court of Shadows, but I at least want someone this side of Faerie to know what we're doing. And right now, Cash is the only council member I trust not to tell Kellen. Agrona works her own agenda and if she decided it was in her best interest to slip some information to the Court of Light, she would."

"You have so little faith in vampires. Would you prefer Dre and I left?" Aidan stood, taking offense where there was none. He knew it was true.

"Knock it off, Aidan. You've known Agrona longer than me, am I wrong?" When he sat back down in a huff, I left. He looked tired, strung out and his agitation got the better of him. He didn't deal well with my ridiculous need to put my ass on the line, as he liked to put it, when we were together. The end of our relationship didn't change anything, especially his feelings for me. I tried to keep that in mind when either of us acted like an asshat. "I'll be right back. Then we can finish going over the details okay?"

He grumbled his agreement. I heard Dre pop a bag of blood in the microwave as I closed the door to my apartment. He needed to eat, we all needed to refuel. The pizza I ate definitely did the trick for me, despite the heartburn. I probably should have chewed it. I bolted down the steps, knocking on Cash's door. Relief chased away the indigestion as I heard locks being undone. I rushed through the door, ready to wrap him up in a huge hug and both thank and apologize to him for being my friend.

Only it wasn't Cash or even Nolak who opened the door. I barreled into a leggy redhead with an athletic build that kept its curves and feminity. I vaguely recalled seeing her face back on Winter Island when Cash fought for Alpha and hanging around a couple other pack functions. I'd have known she was pack anyway by the tattoo on the inside of her right forearm, a black and grey wolf howling at the moon with a tear along its side, exposing ribs made of Celtic knots, all of it encased in a triquetra. The simple trefoil knot represented the man, his wolf and the pack.

The tattoo on her other arm was equally impressive, overlapping black and grey feathers shaping out a leg down to a traditionally drawn paw with claws. If I had to guess, a tribute to her Indian heritage. Add in her Irish features and she was a deadly combination of beauty and bravery. It was no surprise she was in the Salem pack. We'd never been formerly introduced. The look on her face told me she knew who I was. And already decided she didn't like me. I wasn't offended, I sort of had that effect on people.

With my hand extended I introduced myself properly. "I'm Maurin. I live upstairs. I..."

"I know who you are, Maurin.You're friend to the pack, remember? We make it a point to know the people under our protection." She took my proffered hand doing her best to hide her dislike. "I'm Jules, pack healer. You've certainly kept me busy these last few months."

She definitely had good reason not to like me. Trouble follows me around like my shadow. As the pack doctor she cleaned up the mess I tended to leave behind. Jules never moved out of the way to give me full access to the apartment. We stood there, sizing each other up in awkward silence, until Cash walked out of his bedroom.

"Maurin. I was going to stop by in a couple hours. Thought you were still out of it." He scratched his scalp, running fingers through his bed head. "Come on in. I'll put on some coffee."

Jules's eyes glazed over, a soft smile creeping across her face as she watched him pad barefoot into the kitchen. And then it hit me. The real reason she didn't like me. She had a thing for her alpha and he had a crush on me. I tried to separate my feelings for Cash as a friend and see what she saw.

Claw marks across his chest and back marred an otherwise perfect physique.

His pack tattoo took up the majority of his left shoulder, pack magic removed the Boston tattoo that resided there before - something that only happened with alphas. Pack members who left one pack for another were forced to go through a painful process of cutting the tattooed skin away before a new pack tattoo could be placed somewhere else on the body. A pack never tattooed the same flesh as the previous pack.

Cash's rugged good looks and a boy next door smile, which he unfortunately wasted on me, were polar opposite of the fierce wolf I'd come to know and respect. Damn it all, Cash was a looker and he needed to stop wasting his time with me. Jules might actually be his mate and he'd never know it if he kept blocking his wolf with stupid human emotions. He could certainly do worse than a strong, beautiful woman devoted to the pack. I decided right then and there to play matchmaker and take myself, and unfortunately the pack, out of the picture. They needed a happy and healthy alpha more than I needed their help.

"Don't bother with the coffee, I can't stay. Listen, don't worry if you don't see me for a few days." Or weeks, I thought to myself. Who knew how much time would pass out here while we were in Faerie? "I think my father and Mason are being held by Queen Tianna in the Court of Light. We're setting a trap by accepting her offer." I held my hand up to stop his objections. "I know, I know. It's dangerous and stupid. It's the best we've got. I've gotta run. I'll catch up with you when I get back."

Cash made it to the door before I could haul ass upstairs. "Hang on a second." He grabbed my hand, tugging me into the doorway. I hovered there with one foot in his apartment and one foot out in the hallway. "Who's 'we'? Aidan and Dre? You trust the two of them to get you out of Faerie? Without Aidan making some other bargain? You're already in to him for dinner. Next time the price will be higher, your body, your blood. Not gonna happen. You're under my protection. If you're going, we're going."

"No, Cash, you're not." I caught Jules watching us, but didn't say anything. It was as much for her as it was for him. "Even if the king didn't have a fae who can control your wolf at his disposal, I wouldn't risk the pack."

"Damn it, Maurin, you need my help." Cash tried to pull me to him. I pressed a hand against his chest in an effort to keep some distance between us. "You need me."

"Your pack needs you more. I've been a terrible friend, to you and the pack. I'm selfish and I've leaned on you too hard. I realize that now. So I'm going to say what I should have said a long time ago. You're the alpha. That comes before everything, especially me."

Cash cast a glance over his shoulder at Jules before moving us out into the hallway and closing the door behind him. "What's wrong with you? What are you trying to do, get rid of me? Because it won't work."

"I'm not getting rid of you. I'm reminding you of what's more important."

"I don't need you to remind me. I know what's important to me."

"What's more important to your wolf? The pack or me?"

"My wolf is a part of me, Maurin, it doesn't control me or make all the decisions."

"Maurin, we need you up here." Aidan called down from my landing. I looked up at the stairs and back at Cash.

"He snaps his fingers and you go running? Nothing's changed. I feel bad for Mason. At least I liked him."

I pulled Cash into a hug, whispering in his ear. "Everything has changed. That's the whole point. I've found my mate in Mason. I won't stop until I find him and my father. You should listen to your wolf more. He knows what's best for you. Like a leggy redhead in your apartment."

"This isn't the time to play matchmaker." Even while he held onto me, I could tell he was considering what I said about Jules. The wolf already recognized the potential mate in her, the man just saw it for the first time.

"I've got to go." I slipped out of the embrace and poked a finger in his chest, over his heart. "You know I'm right, in here. Just think about what I said."

"This sounds an awful lot like good bye, Maurin. What are you really planning?"

"It's not good bye. We're family. And when you realize I'm right, I'd appreciate it if you'd explain that to Jules."

"Maurin, I'm sorry to keep interrupting. If you're going through with this plan, we need to finish planning it." Aidan's voice carried his impatience down the stairway.

"I don't think he's sorry at all." Cash smiled, shaking his head. "If you get in trouble, call me. I mean it."

"If the king gets control of you, he gets control of the pack."

Cash faced the door, ready to go back inside. "I'm letting you go, Maurin, give me that much. If you get into trouble call, the pack will answer." He went inside without looking back.

Cash was right, it felt a lot like good bye. And in a way, it was. I headed back to my apartment, my heart and mind heavy from what I'd just done and the things I still had to do.

17

"Agrona is our best chance. You're going to have to trust her. We need to alert the king. You can't take on both courts." Aidan tapped his cell phone, waiting to make the call. He never asked me about my conversation with Cash or complain that I smelled like a dog. He'd listened at the top of the stairs. Satisfied there was one less person in his way to win back my affections, he focused solely on the task at hand:stopping Tianna from starting another war between the courts and saving Mason and my father.

"How are you still this loyal to her? She demoted you, gave me your job. You earned that position, you deserved the position. You still do. She basically put me in charge of you."

"I think we can both agree you're not in charge of me, unless we're talking about your bedroom. Then I'm all too happy to succumb to your will." Aidan chuckled, continuing before I could remind him he'd spent his last night in my bedroom a while ago. "She demoted me because I forced her hand. I made a play to keep you safe, to keep you away from Caligula and Bathory. I should have known better. If Agrona let that go, she'd be met with opposition. You may not believe it, but she made the right choice. You are a better team leader than I was. You listen to your team, value our input."

"Aidan, I know what you're trying to do. There are three things Agrona cares about: herself, Kedehern and her position on the Council. Kellen is on the Council."

"You haven't always seen Agrona at her best. I assure you, she cares for those under her protection. She's a fair leader. Firm, but fair." Dre reached across the table, clasping my hand.

Amalie and I rolled our eyes. She'd been there for my indoctrination into council life and as liaison saw firsthand the type of relationship Agrona and I had. "The first night I met her she kicked my ass. That sort of set the tone for our relationship. Since then, she's been all too happy to put my ass on the line. Are you sure she won't side with Tianna? If she does, she'll hand me over to the queen. And the queen will find a way to make me help her."

"The Faerie queen already found a way to convince you. Your father and your lover. Aidan's right, Maurin. You've always listened to your team, you need to listen to us now. Call Agrona."

I caught Aidan's grimace when Dre used the word lover instead of Mason's name, a gentle reminder of who spent time in my bedroom now. Dre's neutrality where Aidan and I were concerned proved I could rely on him. His century long friendship with my ex never impaired his judgment or ability to take orders from me. So, much to Aidan's frustration, I listened when he suggested I call the head of the Council.

"Give me your cell." I held a hand out expectantly to Aidan, opening and closing it in that "give me it" gesture since I didn't have mine on me. I hoped it was on my nightstand or something because I really didn't feel like going back to the Court of Shadows to find it.

"I say call and you give me a song and dance about trusting Agrona. He says call and 'it's give me your phone'? Really?"

I shrugged my shoulders. "Do you want me to call or not?"

"You're incorrigible." Aidan swiped the screen in a complicated pattern to unlock the phone before placing it in my hand.

"True, I'm not sure why this still comes as a surprise to you." I dialed Agrona's number and refilled my coffee mug while I waited for her to answer.

"Hello." The one word came out in a sigh, like she'd already grown tired of a conversation that hadn't even started yet.

"Good evening, Agrona." I leaned a hip against the counter, taking a sip of my coffee.

"Maurin, this is an unexpected surprise, you calling from Aidan's phone. Does this mean the two of you are an item again?" She sounded interested, excited by the prospect of having affairs to meddle in.

"Actually, no. Mason and I are still very much a thing."

"Ah well, Kellen mentioned something about his disappearance. I thought you'd decided to give up the search and find comfort in the arms of an old flame. I took it upon myself to send the rest of your team ahead to the next blood coven location, seeing how you're otherwise indisposed."

Amalie nudged Aidan, mouthing a silent warning that she'd hex his ass if this phone call backfired before I could give him my 'I told you so look'. Kellen fed Agrona enough useless information for her to feel like she knew what was going on, to stay on her good side and make it harder to convince her to betray him. What she left unsaid was her irritation that I hadn't told her myself and that I'd inadvertently directed Council resources into aiding me in the search for my father and Mason. I'd receive more than a reprimand from her if I survived the double cross in the Court of Light.

Aidan handpicked and trained the team long before I took over. This wasn't their first blood coven, they knew the drill. None of that stopped me from worrying. I hadn't reviewed the plans, prepared the case folders or scoped the location. Mahalia's newfound freedom and deadly magic meant my team was in danger. A danger they didn't know waited for them. And Agrona sent them there without the three strongest members of our team as a reminder of who I worked for. It was a petty and vindictive move, one that I would have flipped out over if there was more time. And she didn't know Mahalia escaped.

"Where's the coven located? When did they head out?" I gripped the phone tighter, the plastic cracking under the pressure. Aidan gave me a sympathetic look. He'd been in a similar position a few months ago when he chose me over his team and responsibility to the Council. In hind sight, he made the wrong choice, since we're not together anymore. As far as Agrona was concerned, I'd done the same thing when I failed to retrieve my team from Risqué and shut down the blood covens.

"They should be arriving in Lawrence shortly. And before you get all indignant, yes I alerted them to the possibility of Mahalia's presence. Though I doubt she'd risk capture by lingering at a crime scene. Let's stop pretending you called me about your job and get to the real reason for this conversation." Ever efficient, the vampire queen wasted no time with idle chitchat.

So Kellen fed her the same bullshit story about the King breaking Mahalia out of Faerie prison. That complicated things even more. Worried Agrona would betray me, I decided to keep the information I gave her to a minimum.

"I need your help, Agrona." I gripped the phone tighter, the glass on the screen cracking.

"Of course you do. You're clearly in over your head with the blood covens, the disappearance of your father and the hunter. Kellen informed me of the many attempts on your life. What have you done to incur the wrath of both courts?" She enjoyed making me squirm.

"Honestly, I think it started when I was born."

She laughed, amused by the sincerity she heard in my voice. "What do you require? Despite your dereliction of duty, I'm in a good mood and feeling helpful."

"I need to get a message to the Court of Shadows, to King Ballard. A message for his ears only." I held my breath, waiting for her answer. She was a smart woman. She knew that I'd not only asked her to send word to the king, but to keep the information from Kellen.

"And the message?" Agrona wanted to know before she agreed.

"Your word that the king will hear it and no one else?" Aidan and Dre nodded, encouraging me to continue, even though she hadn't promised anything. I hesitated.

"Don't insult her, Maurin. She's going to help you." Dre whispered like his queen couldn't hear him.

"Ah, Dre is with you as well. I wondered what became of him when he didn't arrive with the rest of the team. I should have known he succumbed to your charms. How is it all the best men fall at your feet? I'll send the message, Maurin. Who the king shares the information with is entirely up to him."

"Tell him things aren't what they seem." I gave her the message and ignored her jab about Dre, knowing full well I wouldn't convince her that we were friends and nothing more.

"That's it? That's the message? Things aren't what they seem? A bit cryptic don't you think?" The mic on her phone picked up the sound of a calligraphy pen scratching across paper. She hand wrote a note to the king and no doubt sealed it with her official crest. Her mark embedded into the red wax still carried weight. It would be delivered by one of Agrona's personal assistants.

"That's enough. He'll know what it means." I loosened my hold on the phone. The tension left my shoulders knowing she'd help.

"My assistant Cherie is taking care of it." She snapped her fingers. The muffled sounds of someone quickly entering and leaving the room came through the phone. Cherie moved with lightning speed. She'd been with Agrona for half a century, quickly gaining her queen's trust. I'd met her only once, the night she gave the stone of Fal to Agrona. The night I met Scota and my fae magic was released. It seemed like a lifetime ago. For all the shit that happened since then, it should have been a lifetime ago.

"Thank you, Agrona." I almost disconnected the call when I heard her voice again.

"Don't thank me yet. There's still the matter of the blood covens. You are the Regulator. Handpicked by the Council to remove the trash from our district. I expect you to clean this up. Tonight." The council chair and queen of the vampires hung up. She had nothing left to say. My father and Mason were irrelevant as far as she was concerned.

"Well, step one of your plan is complete. Now, for step two. So how do we get to the Court of Light?" Amalie wanted to go to Faerie, which told me how much she still feared going up against Mahalia.

"We're going to Lawrence first." Aidan locked eyes with me, daring me to argue. He lost.

"We're going to the Court of Light." It was my turn to stare him down, so I gave him my best Clint Eastwood eyes. Dirty Harry would have been proud.

"You don't know for certain Queen Tianna has them and if she does that she's keeping them at court. As much as it pains me to say it, I think Agrona is right. The blood coven must be our first priority." Aidan never blinked, which wasn't all that impressive given he's a vampire and they don't need to blink as often as the rest of us. Still, he usually took the time to maintain human appearances. He held my gaze, not to hypnotize me, to prove how serious he was.

"It pains you to say it? Does it really?" I did my best to remain calm, yelling at him wouldn't solve anything. I struggled to keep my voice neutral.

Aidan stepped up when I needed help, because he still felt something for me. He'd hoped to pick up the pieces when we found Mason's body. I hadn't given up the search, declared him dead, and that confounded the vampire. Aidan believed we could find a way around the feeding, that the addiction to my blood was the only thing really keeping us apart. He'd never be as vested in finding Mason as I would.

Or even my father for that matter - Arawn barely tolerated my relationship with Aidan. How far would he really go to bring Mason and my father back to me? Was this where we parted ways?

"I can see the doubt creeping into your eyes, Maurin, and it grieves me to know your faith in me is gone. You think so little of me that you believe I'd choose the blood coven over Mason and your father? That I'd sentence them to death for my gain?" Aidan's eyes softened, the determined glare replaced with sadness. "Everything I've done since the first moment I saw you in Mahalia's living room has been with you in mind. You asked for my help, to find the man who stole your heart from me when we were most vulnerable and I still said yes. A lesser man would have turned their back. I couldn't walk away. When you hurt, I share your pain. My heart breaks with yours. I can't walk away, not when it is in my power to help you, to ease your heartache."

Aidan cupped my face as a single tear rolled down my cheek, brushing it away when it reached his thumb. "I need you to think. To think with your head and not your heart. Say we do it your way, we go to Faerie first. We're there one day, maybe two. No problem, right? What if we're gone a year? Time will not be our friend in Faerie. How much damage could Mahalia do this side of Faerie if we're gone that long? Your father and Mason are fae, the Wild Hunt, immortal and Tianna does not possess the only relic known to survive the last fae war that can kill any of our kind. You do. The queen needs them alive. She won't kill them until they've served their purpose:luring you in."

"There are things worse than death, Aidan. You know that as well as I do. She's torturing them. The longer they stay with her, the less like themselves they'll be when I get them back."

"We don't know that. We have no reason to believe any harm has come to them. How long do you think the Salem coven will be able to with stand Mahalia's dark magic? How long before the norms fall at her feet? For the love of blood, you don't even know what the queen wants you to do. What if going to her first ensures their death, the death of everyone we care about?"

"What if we're only in Faerie a few minutes? I could make the same arguments." I swallowed hard, forcing the pizza making its way back up my throat down. The thought of what I was about to say, the idea of leaving Mason and my father with Tianna any longer made me sick. Once again, Aidan was right and that was really getting on my nerves.

"We go to Lawrence first. If Mahalia's not there, we go to Faerie when we're through with the blood coven. We don't go to the next suspected location, we don't chase the witch. She's a pawn in Tianna's game. I know it. Misdirection and a way to split us up. She bet that Agrona would give the order to take out the coven first and that I'd go off on my own. And yes, I am aware that six months ago that probably would have worked."

The smallest possibility remained that I was wrong about everything. I didn't have any hard evidence Tianna had

Arawn and Mason, just a gut feeling. Which just as easily could be indigestion. Lawrence was the smart move, the only move we could make with any certainty. Which just solidified my suspicions that we were being played.

18

Lawrence looked like any other city struggling to find the funds for necessary improvements in a bad economy. The only businesses booming were drugs and guns. A perfect breeding ground for blood magic, far more fertile than Danvers or Salem. Apartment buildings blocked out the sky and created channels for the air to build up speed, making it colder and windier than the suburbs.

The neighborhood, once dominated by Italians, became a mixture of Latino and Russian immigrants over the years. Devout Catholic families struggling to make ends meet and hold onto their community until one day, the thread they were holding onto broke and the gangs took over; ran the families out of town, the ones who could leave at least, and set up shop. Needles and trash took the place of tumbleweed in this desolate section of the city. An urban wasteland. Boarded up row home after row home, squatters scurrying down the alleys.

Eight blocks over, you'd find Tripoli bakery, one of the last bastions of hope for the Chamber of Commerce and home of some of the best cookies you'll ever eat in your life. Too bad we weren't here for baked goods. I'd much rather be working in the renovated part of town.

I stepped over a guy passed out on the sidewalk, dropping a few quarters in the cup next to his Vietnam veteran sign and headed for the gypsy Esna's shop. She sold fortunes, forties and lottery tickets in the front while her nephews ran drugs out of the back. I'd had a run-in with her back when I worked with SPTF.

Matthison and I tracked a seer who'd been accused of using his gifts for financial gain to her store, The Palm of Your Hand. The trail went cold shortly after that. Everyone knew Esna moved people in and out of town. By the time we got there, our perp was long gone, heard he got picked up in Portland. Some people never learn.

Esna's family ran the ten blocks surrounding the rundown Tune and Lube Agrona sent my team to check out. We'd messaged Jasmina that we were on our way, but hadn't heard back. We needed some intel. If anybody knew what went down around here, it was Esna.

The Palm of Your Hand smelled like cheap incense and cheaper booze with a hint of stale cigar smoke. A beaded curtain separated Esna's part of the store from her cousin's. My hand hovered over the old fashioned bell on the counter, ready to announce our presence, when a heavily tattooed hand parted the curtain. Glass beads swayed and clicked together as she walked through.

The self-proclaimed great and powerful mystic leaned on the counter, her faded, orange afghan shawl and powder blue housecoat struggling to contain the large woman inside. She'd put on a few years and more than a few pounds. Esna waited to hear why I'd come back to her shop after her explicit instructions for me not to do so. Our first and last visit didn't exactly end on a positive note. Thankfully, Aidan had a few Benjamins in his pocket that would convince her to talk.

The gypsy gave my friends the once over, realizing very quickly we weren't here on police business when no one waved a badge in her face. She looked nervous. I chalked it up to having two vampires, a witch and one badass dog at my back. Nothing against Matthison, he was tough, but Esna knew he followed the book. The people who stood before her were more likely to beat her into unconsciousness with the book than follow it.

"I told you not to show your face around here again, cop. You're cursed, trouble follows you around. I burned ten pounds of sage after you left just to get the bad juju out. Still stinks in here. And now you're back, leaking your toxic aura all over the place. Besides, I ain't done nothing, so I got nothing to say."

And there was the reason our introduction didn't go so well the last time.

Matthison warned me before he took me inside not to cause a scene. I lost my cool somewhere around the toxic aura. Esna lied to her clients, she wasn't a seer. She knew we were coming because she saw us on the security cameras not because she saw into the future. A fraud when it came to fortunes, there was no doubt about it. However, she did have one unique skill.

Esna knew if you were an Other. No matter the glamour or how vehemently you denied it, she knew. And she did not approve of my position with SPTF. She went out of her way to let me know it. Long story short, drawing your weapon and threatening to shoot her in the knee cap was not the best way to get information from Esna. I planned on using a different approach the second time around.

"I'm not here to talk about you or the pharmaceuticals your cousins are running out the back. Just want to ask you some questions. See if you've heard anything about a new coven in town."

"Who wants to know? That two-bit police department you work for? Bunch of racist pricks. I don't know how they managed to convince two vampires and a witch to work for them. Is that your Faerie dog? He can't be in here. It's a health code violation."

I held back a laugh. Like she gave a shit about health code violations. "I'm not with SPTF. I work for the Council now. And they have a few questions about a blood coven."

"Blood coven, huh? You after a witch or something?" She held out her hand, so that we could clearly see the green dollar sign with the words 'pay up sucker' tattooed on her palm.

I nodded to Aidan who grudgingly got out his wallet and laid a crisp hundred dollar bill on her calloused hand. Vampires never paid for information. Something he reminded me of at least ten times on the way over. I reminded him that we might have to come back and we'd need her again if we did. I also reminded him that I'd only recently experienced a bank account with a balance in the black and that he'd had a couple lifetimes to accumulate his wealth when he asked why he was the one paying the gypsy.

Esna ran her thumb along the new bill, enjoying the feel of freshly minted money, before holding it up to the light to check for water marks and the security strip. Satisfied we weren't passing off counterfeit money, she folded it up and tucked it in her bra. "I may have seen some shady people coming and going from the Tune and Lube across the street. They didn't look like no grease monkeys either, if you know what I'm saying."

"What did they look like? Did you see an old woman with them?" Amalie stepped out from behind Aidan so Esna could get a better look at her, and have direct eye contact should she need to bespell the gypsy.

"What about a couple of vampires? And a werewolf? Maybe a fire starter? Have you seen any of them around? Maybe in the last couple of hours?" Dre threw a few of his own questions out.

"I'm not sure. Maybe." Esna held out her hand again. She planned to squeeze us for every dollar Aidan had.

"If you could be a little more specific, we'd greatly appreciate it." His words were professional and polite, but the warning was impossible to miss. He placed another hundred in her hand, pressing hard enough with one finger to dent her meaty palm and disrupt the circulation.

"I saw some people poking around a little while ago. I called my cousin because Mr. Al has been under family protection since I was this high." She held her hand up to her waist in a gesture that related height to age. "He told me it was nothing, not to worry about it. So I didn't. Since you're asking, something ain't right with those witches Mr. Al is subletting to. And those people I seen poking around? They went in and they ain't come back out."

Aidan set a cool grand on the counter. "If anyone else comes around asking questions, you didn't see us, you didn't see anything." When she only nodded, he leaned in and whispered something about centuries ago, promised the things in the night that chased gypsy coaches across Europe would return if she betrayed us. "Now, are we clear Esna?"

With wide eyes and a healthy dose of fear, the tough as nails con artist replied, "Crystal."

I asked Aidan to tell me exactly what he said to Esna as we walked out of her shop, the chime on the door dinging behind us. He evaded my questions with promises to tell me the story over dinner and drinks. A little reminder of my promise to him.

An old donut shop sat just down the street from the Tune and Lube. I knew from experience the donuts weren't fresh and neither was the coffee. At least the owner kept the place pretty clean. What it lacked in culinary quality it made up for in view. Specifically of the lot around the garage.

Conry did his fading trick, easily slipping inside without the girl behind the counter noticing him. Amalie and I grabbed a booth by the big front windows while Aidan and Dre ordered for us.

Sitting still was impossible. Moving gave me something to focus on, the road, the plan, our target. When we idled my mind drifted to dark places. Every way to torture a person I knew of ran through my mind, all the ways Mason suffered while I did nothing. The table shook from my uncontrollable foot tapping, spilling the coffee when Aidan set it down. Amalie grabbed napkins from the holder and wiped up the mess before adding four creamers to her mug. Aidan slid onto the bench seat next to me, forcing my knee to stop bobbing. He didn't say anything, neither did Dre. They'd both been where I was before. So we sat there in silence, watching the lot across the street.

"You could send Conry over. Nobody would see him like that." Conry's head was in my lap as soon as Dre suggested it.

"He can't stay like this for long when he's not close to me. It's not a good idea." I blew him off, no way was Conry going over there.

"Of course it is. It's bloody brilliant. What's the matter with you," Dre asked, pointing at me. "You're losing it, kid."

"I just got him back. What if he can't cloak long enough? I just got him away from them." I refused to be separated from Conry. He'd been by my side ever since we found him tortured and abused in the basement of that house in Danvers.

"We just need him to scope out the place. Take a look around and come back." Dre stuck to his guns.

"He's a Cwnn Anfwnn, not Lassie. How do you expect him to tell you what he sees? So far my conversations with him have been pretty one sided."

"He just goes over there, pokes around. If it's clear, he makes himself visible and we go over there. If not, he comes back and we figure out another way. Sitting here staring at a parking lot full of used tires and scrap car parts isn't helping anybody. Especially you, Maurin." Dre sat back in the booth, arms crossed over his chest, confident he was right and the others would agree.

I searched my other friends' faces, looking for reassurance that they were not expecting me to risk Conry. Amalie looked out the window, studying the lot and avoiding my eyes. She agreed with Dre. Aidan handed me my coffee and pushed the raspberry jelly donut I'd asked for in front of me. My fingers shook just a little when I picked it apart, dipping a piece of the raised donut's dry edge into the center. He didn't push, just gave me the time to come to the conclusion that Dre's plan was the best option we had.

I mindlessly picked at my donut until a few crumbs remained. Aidan watched, hunger and desire flared in his eyes as my tongue ran along the corner of my mouth, cleaning away a drop of raspberry jelly. Something stirred in him at the sight of me licking the red stickiness from my face. Aware for the first time his hand was still on my thigh, stroking the inner seam of my jeans, I squirmed in my seat alerting Conry to my discomfort. A growl, soft enough to escape human ears and loud enough for a vampire's, rumbled from his chest. Aidan stilled, a look of hunger darkened his face, not for my blood, for all of me. I wondered how many times he'd dreamed of turning me, how close I'd come to becoming his eternal love while we were together.

"Forgive me. I..."

"Nothing to forgive, Aidan. It's not like you bit me or something."

Amalie watched the tense exchange in confusion, but Dre knew his friend well. He recognized how close I'd come to having more than jelly stains on my face.

"Aidan, you want to step out, get some fresh air?" Dre pulled a Cuban out of his coat pocket, snipping the end with his gold cigar cutter. He picked up the habit before I was born. When I asked why he smoked, he explained that he'd lost his palate for food and drink, his taste buds dead to everything except blood. His sense of smell had only improved when he became a vampire. He remembered the smell of pipe tobacco on his father when he was a little boy. Smoking kept him connected to a part of his lost humanity. And he couldn't get cancer.

"No, we're fine. Everything is fine. I can't have you out there smoking and one of the coven spot you." The truth was we all could use the fresh air. There were enough pheromones floating around to turn everyone in the donut shop into a fang banger. We couldn't risk them giving us away.

"Then I suggest you come up with a plan before Aidan makes one for you. The life altering kind, if you catch my drift. Breathing all this Faerie isn't good for anyone." Resigned to the fact that he wasn't getting a smoke break, he gnawed on the end of the cigar. "You reek of it. Ever since your trip to the dark court."

"I stink?" Suddenly self-conscious, I turned my head to do the discrete pit check.

The door opened, setting off the electronic chime to alert the staff of a new customer, except no one came through. No one left either. The latch clicked and the girls behind the counter went back to texting and tweeting, everything except brewing fresh coffee or replenishing the case with fresh donuts. The closed door held our attention. The whole table poised for an attack.

"I don't sense magic. A few faint traces from across the street. Nothing else." Amalie smoothed the static from her hair.

I felt something, a tug on my chi and the power I'd spindled there. Conry. My right palm slapped against the window, a sheet of cold safety glass the only thing separating me from my dog. He'd gone across the street in stealth mode to check out the garage. Fog formed on the window from my breath, my face pressed against it as I kept watch on my guardian. He knew I wouldn't let him go and went anyway. My father was right, my stubbornness rubbed off on him. In the relatively short time he'd been in my care, I'd undone his breeding and a lifetime of training.

Anxiety tightened my chest and strained my breathing. Saving Conry saved my sanity. I wouldn't have been able to keep it together if all three of them were still missing. And now the one thing holding my breakdown at bay was poking around a faction of the blood coven who tried to kill him. I swiped my hand across the glass, clearing away the condensation so I could see better. It didn't do much, my vision blurred from the tears threatening to fall as the stress of the situation and the exhaustion from holding on to the hope that my father and Mason lived reached its peak.

Conry's bark broke through the tense silence. I turned from the window, ready to shove Aidan out of the bench seat so I could go to Conry. Still in tune to my thoughts and emotions, he was already up. He stood in the aisle between the counter and our table with his hand extended. I took it, letting him pull me across the formica seat.

I bolted out the door as soon as my feet hit the linoleum. The chime above the door dinged again, Aidan, Dre and Amalie hot on my heels. The sprint across the street felt like the Boston Marathon, time seems to slow when you are trying to reach a loved one. My heart pounded, a toxic mix of adrenaline and fear. Conry revealed himself and sounded an alarm, barking to let us know it was clear. That meant no coven. What if I was wrong, what if Mason and my father were inside, dead at the hands of Mahalia and her blood witches and the queen never had them? I whistled for Conry, swallowing my doubts once he was beside me.

The metal garage bay doors were closed and locked from the inside. Aidan and Dre stood on opposite corners, ready to rip one down when I suggested we try around back. "We paid Esna off. Not the whole town. People will notice two vampires ripping a garage apart. Like those two airheads behind the counter at the donut shop with a clear view across the street. There's got to be a door around back."

"Excuse me." Amalie nudged her way between the vampires. With a snap of her fingers chain clanked against concrete inside the garage and the bay door popped up enough for us to slide it up and back along the rails with hardly a sound. She went inside, snapping again for effect as two of the old shop lights flickered on. "It's nothing, no need to thank me." She quickly spun around to face us, the satisfaction in her eyes didn't match the horror in ours.

Conry and I walked over to her. "No one will blame you if you want to go outside." I held onto to her as she struggled to turn around.

"What are you talking about? Go outside for what?" She'd looked and still hadn't seen anything when the lights came on, turning around too fast for her brain to process anything.

Her job as liaison was a little different than when I held the position. She spent her hours on the Council's time clock, meeting with Mason or another representative from SPTF, filing reports and handling press releases or conferences. She saw more than most witches her age. None of which came close to this. Things are different in the heat of battle. You choose not to recognize the faces of the fallen as you charge on to defeat the enemy.

This wasn't like the time we fought together against a demon army. This wasn't a battle it was the aftermath. Over the years as an interrogator for SPTF and now as the Regulator, I'd learned how to compartmentalize. To shove the dark, horrible things I see people do into a box deep inside my mind and lock it away. It changes you and I didn't want that for Amalie.

I fought to hold on to her, even as her skin became increasingly hotter. She was determined to see what we saw, to know what happened. Amalie's hair began to stand on end as she pulled her power to her and electrified her body. High voltage reverberated through me from head to toe, rattling my teeth, forcing me to let go of her. A quick intake of breath, the only sign of her shock as she took in the horror around her. For the first time, Amalie faced the ugly truth of what her mentor became. A dark, twisted soul. A woman capable of turning her back on the creed and her religion, of the foulest magic and torture. Small tremors radiated outward from Amalie in the air and through the concrete floor, a physical manifestation of her anger at what Mahalia's new coven had done.

I hadn't seen anything like this since the Inquisitors were killed by the Afrit. A case I worked for SPTF and the coven. The same case Mahalia betrayed me on and tried to kill me. Aidan noticed the similarities in the pattern of blood spray inside the garage as well. He'd been brought in on the case, before we knew we were dealing with the nastiest level of djinn, as an expert in vampiric messages or clues hidden with a victim's blood spatter on the walls. He stood back, trying to decipher any words or pictures hidden in the void where blood hadn't soaked the walls.

I moved cautiously through the room in an attempt to avoid disturbing the scene. Body parts littered the floor. It was a massacre. I'd already sent Masarelli and Agrona a group text that we were on site and to notify Lawrence's task force. The words to describe what happened to our comrades escaped me. There was no way to describe what I saw in a text.

I dropped my head, whispering a prayer to all the gods listening for Mahalia to be brought to justice and typed the words 'the team is dead'. Alerts came through seconds after my text was received. A cleanup crew and crime scene technicians were on their way. We had minutes to get what information would could and get out of there.

"You will know pain." Aidan found the message in the drying blood of our fire witch.

"She did this. She did this to a witch that used to follow her." Amalie's voice quivered, tears ran down her face.

"We don't have any evidence Mahalia was here. She's at court with the queen." I looked at Aidan, that last part meant for him. He agreed if I came here first instead of going to court, for Mason and my father, that we wouldn't chase false leads if Mahalia wasn't here. She wasn't. She was at court with Tianna.

"It doesn't matter. She sanctioned the torture and murder of a council-appointed team. She tortured and killed witches. I need to call Oberon. I'm going to step outside." Amalie finally reached the point of no return. Mahalia was a dead woman.

"You can't bring her to court." Dre recognized the power still bound inside Amalie for the first time. "She'll lose control."

"Oberon broke the bonds Mahalia placed on Amalie when he took over the coven. She's keeping all of that energy in check on her own. She's all about control." I watched Amalie pace in front of the garage door while she talked to Oberon. "She should be running the coven."

"If she takes down the crone she could. Others will follow her where they wouldn't Oberon. He is still tainted by

Mahalia in the coven's eyes. Even more so with his failure to stop the blood covens for taking root in Salem. A little young, but even-tempered and fair. She would make a good priestess." Aidan would be making a recommendation to the Council when this was over. I had a hunch the position for liaison would be opening up soon.

"So we're in agreement? We're going to court?" I prepped myself for jumping so many. It exhausted a lot of energy to move four people and a Cwnn Anfwnn through the Between.

"When you said we were going to Faerie if Mahalia wasn't here, I didn't realize you meant we'd be leaving right from here. I didn't pack. I'm under armed." Dre pulled out one glock and one extra clip with saltwater ammo.

"That's all you brought?" I walked over to the Camaro parked across the street, popping the trunk once everyone caught up.

Amalie gave a low whistle. "Damn Aidan. You've got an arsenal in your trunk."

"Don't look at me. She did this." Aidan jabbed a thumb in my direction. "I let her use my car and this is how I got it back. Cash's influence no doubt."

"I didn't hear you complaining when we had the hollow points made from melted crosses on our last job. Or the mini cross bow with rowan wood arrows." I outfitted the trunk with everything we needed from saltwater to holy water. It was a thing of beauty. Unfortunately it was ill-equipped for fighting fae. Two iron daggers, plus a few sets of iron cuffs and shackles were all I could find.

"I don't have much for Faeries. I was thinking, we shouldn't go in loaded up with iron anyway. It'll tip them off. Normal ammo still hurts them." I stepped aside so they could load up. I had the only weapon I needed. The Retaliator.

19

"Do you even know how to get into the Court of Light?" Dre took another drag of his cigar, smoke coiling around him like a snake.

"Of course I do. Shut up. And put that damn thing out would you. You're tainting the Between. It makes it harder to focus." I decided against jumping all four of us directly to Faerie, electing to pull back the veil and slip us into the grey instead. Kind of like a pit stop. I'd only been to the Hall of Illusion, not the actual court. Trying to take all of us somewhere I've never been seemed like too much of a risk. Someone would get left behind or worse, stuck. Not to mention jumping from here cost less energy and I needed all the strength I had. Tianna wasn't just going to let me walk out with my father and Mason.

My body became a conduit. In the Between, I didn't rely on stored energy. Power flowed through me, from me into the things I manifested. I imagined a place, gilded and gleaming in light. A queen bright and beautiful on her throne, surrounded by subjects. A tad cliché, it was the best I could do under the circumstances. It's really seventy-five percent intention anyway. The details are to help with focus, visualize your destination so you arrive there. In my lessons with Mason, I'd advanced beyond needing the visual aids. I simply thought about where I wanted to go, focused on words and less pictures. I'd come a long way from deconstructing and rebuilding places in my mind in order to jump. My movements in the Between were faster, smoother and without hesitation. Of course those places weren't in the ever changing, magic based Faerie.

"Brace yourselves. I can't promise it won't be daylight when we arrive." I gritted my teeth as the flow of energy increased.

"I've been thinking about that. It's not the true sun we see in Faerie, just a magical manipulation. So I don't think you'll burn." Amalie beamed at the vampires.

Aidan and Dre weren't as confident in Amalie's new theory as they were in the shadow spell she cloaked them in. I wasn't sold on either idea. We didn't have much choice. They agreed to the risk.

The grey slipped away, revealing a familiar landscape. I'd been here before when Scota awoke the Faerie in my blood. Elysium. One and the same as the Court of Light? Not possible. I was no longer the vessel for an ancient goddess, the way to Elysium permanently closed to me. This place had been created in its likeness. I wasn't surprised the queen of light lured her subjects into the illusion they resided in the home of the gods. She believed they were gods, held above all others, even their darker brethren.

The moon, heavy and full, hung in anticipation for its time to shine as the sun slowly crept behind the horizon leaving streaks of purples and pinks in its wake. We all breathed a collective sigh of relief. With the oncoming night there was no need to test Amalie's hypothesis or have our vampires stunted beneath her cloaking spell. Aidan and Dre became more visible as she pulled back on her magic.

"So now what?" Amalie shoved her scarf in her satchel.

Spring hadn't settled in Salem yet, while everything bloomed in Faerie. We'd dressed in layers for the temperature at home. King Ballard would find us easily enough, there'd be a trail of clothes to follow like bread crumbs.

"Honestly I thought we'd trip some kind of alarm or something when we came through. I thought they'd come to us." I shrugged my shoulders, confused by the lack of Faerie guards. I expected different results if we tried this in the dark court.

"I didn't pack for a nature hike. No food, no water. We could be walking for days and we can't rely on the landscape. And before you ask, the only way I can manifest food is by calling for take out." Amalie pulled the sleeves of her coat around her waist, tying them in a tight knot.

"I've been thinking, I don't think it's real hunger or thirst you'll feel in Faerie." Aidan mimicked her voice, mocking her theory.

"Okay, okay. Let's not lose our shit." Dre scratched his jaw. "I'm with Maurin on this one."

"You seem to be with Maurin on a lot things lately." Aidan hid the accusation of Dre's growing feelings for me.

An accusation I knew to be false. Trust, loyalty and friendship, I'd earned those things from Dre working side by side. He was my brother, in arms and in everything else. It didn't go further than that for either of us.

Agrona planted a seed and Aidan had been nurturing it in his mind since I'd talked with her. The look in Dre's eyes was like a drought to a new crop. Aidan's fear of Dre and becoming something else withered away.

Aidan shook his head, then rubbed his temples. "Fucking Faeries and their head games." A small, glittering orb, no bigger than a speck of dust flitted around him until he swatted it away.

"Okay, so we can add that, whatever that was, to the list of stuff we should watch out for while we're here." Amalie inspected Aidan, checking the dilation of his eyes and length of his fangs to be sure he was alright before he shooed her off.

The concern over the desire to spill, or in the case of our vampire friends drink, fae blood was real. They'd both had a taste already and that would only intensify the thirst when we were surrounded by so many at court. I trusted them not to fuck up and give in to a little bloodlust. I didn't bring two newborns along. I brought two hardened professionals who watched my back every time we went after the bad guys.

"Like I was saying before you so rudely interrupted," Dre smiled, relieved his best mate hadn't gone barking mad, "it's weird that no guards came running. Something is up."

"Guards? Why would my queen need guards to retrieve a welcomed guest and her companions?" With a hand at his waist, Kellen half bowed in my direction. "Have you changed your mind about her offer then?"

I didn't miss the darkness in his eyes. Something was up indeed, but this was what we came here for. It was time we got this show on the road.

"I have. Will she see me?" I didn't mince words.

"We were certain we'd see death before we'd see you in the Court of Light. My mistress has been waiting for you." Kellen motioned for us to follow him.

We exchanged puzzled glances behind his back as he led us through the small glade to a copse of trees. The branches, burdened with leaves swayed until the walkway was revealed, the canopy opened up for the moon to light our path. I walked behind Kellen, the feeling of dread gnawing away at my stomach, pondering his words and the worry of what they might mean. I had a hunch he wasn't talking about their own demise when he mentioned seeing death first. Gods help them if Agrona didn't send the message or Ballard didn't show. My friends would not die in another one of my harebrained plans.

I imagined a gleaming ivory castle, with towers so tall the tips of their roofs touched the clouds and banners that whipped in wind. Something a little like Camelot. Not the

Grecian temple that rose before us, etched from marble with massive columns along its front and grape vines growing over the promenade protruding from its side. It felt out of time, out of place, inside Faerie. But then so did I. I belonged to neither court.

If I'd have known I'd spend so much time in Faerie, I'd have bought myself a pocket watch like the one I gave my father. My watch stopped working the moment we crossed over. Digital watches, cell phones and other devices had a tendency to malfunction around so much wild magic. There was no phone a friend option inside Faerie. You got yourself in, you got yourself out. Or you didn't get out at all. Rip Van Winkle didn't sleep his life away in the countryside. He'd been trapped in Faerie by a possessive little garden sprite. Unable to escape, his life passed him by. Until she tired of him and dropped him back in the country where all the years caught up with him and he became a withered old man in a matter of minutes. I possessed two relics where he had had none. I escaped one court only to walk right into another. I prayed for a repeat performance.

20

The moonlight reflected off the white marble walls and columns inside Tianna's court. Much like the great temples her home was modeled after - or more likely the other way around - the building was open on all sides except the back wall where her throne sat. It felt cold, despite the warmer air settling in from outside. Once you looked beyond the magnificent architecture and beautiful marble, the cold settled into your bones and you realized how hardened this court became. Where Ballard's court appalled and terrified, underneath there was still heat and passion within the black walls of his home. Here there was nothing, a vacuum of emotions.

She sat on her throne, ladies in waiting littered the steps leading up to the dais. Tianna looked up from their adoring faces, it was then I realized two of the girls were washing away the grass stains on her bare feet.

"I like to be one with Faerie when I work. It grounds my magic, centers me." She decided her feet were clean enough, flicking one of the girls away with her right foot. Toweled dry and in silver satin slippers, she focused on my visit. "So Kellen tells me you have reconsidered my offer. Am I to assume your men have not been returned to you?"

The queen caught my puzzled gaze. Kellen informing the queen of anything apart from my arrival was news to me.

"As consort to the throne, we share a unique bond. I'm sure you understand the importance of privacy. A queen is afforded so little these days." By privacy she meant secrecy. Everyone knew the cutthroat politics and espionage that took place at court.

"You said you could help me find them and Mahalia?" Actually, her offer was more you scratch my back I'll scratch yours. She never told me what she wanted me to do. It was time to find out. If I wanted to play this out, bluff my way through making her give me my father and Mason back, I needed to know.

"Yes, I believe I did. One good deed deserves another. Isn't that what the mortals say?" She glided down from the dais, her slippers barely making a sound on the steps and floor as she made her way over to me. She slipped her arm through mine, leading me around the room. We'd done this before in the Hall of Illusion. "So you help me with my problem and I'll help you, dear. It's very simple."

"Do you know where they are?" Despite the ploy, the desperation in my voice was real.

"Of course I do dear." She gave my arm a little pat. "It's as I told you before. Don't worry, they're safe for now. So there is the matter I need your help with."

Each of my companions shared a look of concern, telling me to get on with it with their eyes. The longer this took the more likely my father and Mason would be harmed. The less likely we'd get out of Faerie.

"You still haven't told me what that is. I can't help you if you don't tell me the problem." I laid a hand over hers in the crook of my arm.

The repulsion at my touch that flashed across her face was quickly replaced with the mask of kindness and friendship she usually wore. "How silly of me." She stopped walking, turning slightly to face me. "I know you've met Ballard. Seen the disgusting things he is capable of, the monstrosities he has created." She checked the vampires in her peripheral. She counted them among the monsters Ballard made. "I long for things to be like they were."

I nodded my head yes. I met Ballard, visited his court and seen the horrors that happened within those walls. Not all of his creations were monstrous. Just about everything I loved could be traced back to the Court of Shadows - according to Ballard anyway. I'm sure things lurked in the deepest part of his dungeons that would give me nightmares.

Tianna scared the shit out of me, too. I'd be a fool not to be afraid of her. I doubted very much she'd see the comparison.

"You don't need me for that. If you want to reconcile with Ballard, I'm sure he would be amicable to that, willing to set terms for a reunion." I tried to sound hopeful even though I knew having the king back at her side wasn't exactly what she had in mind.

"Don't be absurd. Is she always this way? This oblivious to the obvious?" She looked to my friends for an answer, carrying on before she got one. "I have no desire for Ballard to be at my side. I want one court. Not a unification of courts."

I let that sink in before I spoke, my pace slowing down until she jerked me beside her again. "I want to make sure I understand what you're asking. You want to eradicate the dark court, kill Ballard and you want me to do it. Does that about sum it up?"

"I believe so, yes." Tianna was as nuts as Ballard, insanity ruled both courts.

"That's not possible, it can't be done. I can't do it."

"Some might say it is impossible for a halfling to wield the sword of Manannan, to call relics to her aid, and yet you do. Despite your mixed blood, the Retaliator resonates with power. Can you not hear it, the song of the blade? One of the few weapons fatal to our kind and you hold it. And the charm around your neck. There are some, myself included, who believe you can."

"I sometimes believe as many as six impossible things before breakfast," I said, stealing a line from Alice in Wonderland. "This isn't one of them. You think Ballard will let me get close enough to kill him? You'd have done it yourself if it were that easy."

"If I killed my ex-husband, it would be a declaration of war. If you kill him, it would solidify my reign."

"When you declare me enemy of the crown. You're not making a very good case. I came to you for help and to help you in return. I'd like to actually live to see Mason and my father when this is over."

"Perhaps you're just lacking the proper motivation." She stopped, eyes closed and face upturned toward the sky, never letting go of my arm. In fact, her grip tightened and I barely managed not to wince.

Worry and a little fear marred the faces of my friends. Tianna looked to the heavens while I looked straight at them. Kellen stood behind them with a wicked grin on his face. Rays of sun filled the void between columns before spilling out onto the floor. I watched, terrified as each beam of light crept closer and closer to Aidan and Dre. I muttered curses and prayed that Amalie's theory was correct. This was not the true sun. I murmured it over and over again.

"It matters not. They believe it will burn and so it shall." Tianna's voice was a whisper, her breath hot on my ear. "Watch." She extended a finger, pointed at my vampires. Her hands were like a pianist's, long graceful fingers covered with flawless skin like bone china. Too beautiful to point to such torture.

The faintest shafts of smoke began to rise off their shoulders before they were engulfed in sunlight and consumed by fire. Kellen dragged Conry and Amalie away before they were burned as well. I cried out, begged for her to bring back the darkness, to shroud them in shadows so they could begin to heal. And in that moment, I realized they truly were Ballard's children. I was stupid to think I could bring them here, that Amalie's magic could protect them.

Flames leapt from one vampire to the other. Yellow danced with orange, bursts of white as the heat intensified. Blackened skin cracked off in large flakes, littering the floor around them, exposing new flesh only to be burned again. The older the vampire, the longer it took to die in the sun. Regeneration happened at a faster rate with age, a necessity for longevity. Their bodies healed even while the flames ate at their flesh, prolonging the process. It was why vampires who wanted to die preferred rowan wood stakes or decapitation.

I reached for my sword, prepared to end it. I hadn't decided if I was going to kill her or put my friends out of their misery. Either way it would be over.

Tianna snuffed out the fire. The rays of sun covered under the blanket of night, moonlight the only illumination left in the room. Aidan and Dre collapsed, every inch of them charred and black. Where the skin split open, it exposed raw flesh beneath still trying to heal. Amalie hung from Kellen's grip, limp in his arms as she wept for our friends, certain they were dead. I knew better. Dead would be a pile of ash. This was worse than death. This was a suspended state of torture, agonizing pain, slow almost undetectable healing with no blood. They could be like this for weeks without feeding. I hated that Ballard was right, his estranged wife was no better than him. No wonder my father remained neutral, kept his own court under the radar of the two of them.

"You can end their pain, Maurin, put them out of their misery. They'll find no food here." Tianna's eyes were on the sword in my hands. "Or you can make it so it never was."

"What are you talking about? You did that. Look at them!" My fingers tightened on the hilt of my sword, knuckles white.

"You can. You are more your mother's child than Arawn's. She was the only witch ever born who could harness the Between, manipulate space. Not just space, Maurin, time."

"You're crazy. Even if my mother could do that, it doesn't mean I can."

I caught movement from Amalie's direction in my peripheral. Still in Kellen's grip, she managed to work a spell I was certain bordered on dark magic. Blood dripped at a steady pace from her fingertips pooling in a crimson puddle on the marble floor. A small amount began to run, like branches of a river toward Aidan and Dre. No one noticed. She needed more time. A few drops of blood wouldn't do much in the way of healing their burns, but it would take the edge off their pain.

"How do you know you can't? You haven't even tried, dear." Tianna's casual attitude toward the pain and suffering she'd inflicted on my friends infuriated me.

I raised my sword, the tip inches from the crazed queen. This whole thing went to hell in a hand basket faster than I anticipated. Ballard was MIA. I had no way of knowing if the spies tipped him off to my arrival in the Court of Light or my agreement to help Tianna. Even if Agrona failed to send the message, my presence should have been enough to send the Dark Guard. For the moment, I was on my own. I couldn't kill the queen. The whereabouts of my father and Mason would die with her and she knew it. It was written all over her face.

"I wouldn't do that if I were you." Kellen held Amalie in a different position, her head pulled back with a fist in her hair and a blade pressed against her throat.

"Lower your dagger, Kellen. Maurin isn't going to kill me. She's going to try, try very hard to rid me of my problem. Aren't you, child?" Tianna stepped closer, so close if she breathed heavily she'd prick her skin on the blade. "She wants to see her father and her lover again."

Kellen lowered his dagger, the same wicked look on his face as when I first met him the night he escorted Mahalia to Faerie prison from her trial. He'd been orchestrating this for a very long time. A fae with the patience of a saint, and the desires of a devil. The look in his eye said he planned to finish what he started. He caressed her soft, milky white skin, his fingers trailing down her collar bone to the cleft of her breast before he shoved her to the floor. Amalie landed hard, the knees of her pants soaking up the blood she spilled for Aidan and Dre.

"Stop! I don't know how."

Kellen kicked Amalie in the stomach. The air rushed out of her lungs as she toppled over. "You know how. I've seen you unmake things in the Between. You don't move from one place to the next like the rest of us. You deconstruct it, brick by brick, piece by piece, until nothing is left and then you rebuild again."

"Those are buildings. Inanimate objects in the present time and I only do it that way because I still haven't mastered jumping. Is there some kind of worm hole in the Between I don't know about?" When she said she needed help, I thought she wanted a hitman, typical crazy divorcee shit. But this? Erase the dark court from history? I couldn't even bluff my way through that. There was no way I could hide an entire court long enough for her to think I'd succeeded, while I plotted with Ballard to take her out.

I looked at the blackened heap beside Amalie. Kellen had moved to stand between her and the bodies in an effort to keep her from feeding them again. Small lines of pale pink were visible in the fissures along their burnt flesh, the skin regenerating. The queen's consort made a potentially fatal mistake.

Aidan reached out, flakes of skin floated off his hands as he grabbed Kellen's ankle. Blood flowed freely from the spot where Aidan tore a chunk free. Dre lapped up the potent blood on the floor while I watched my ex suckle the fae flesh until every last drop was consumed. It was only a matter of time before the blood restored the vampires. As close to true death as they were, blood rage was a very real possibility. One that scared me a little. I had fae in my blood. They'd be as crazed for me as everyone at court. Kellen limped away, dragging his injured foot behind him as he joined the queen.

Relieved as I was that they'd be ready to fight, I knew they just sped up the time clock. Tianna realized the vampires weren't going down easily. She'd come to the same conclusion as me. Fae was the flavor of the month when Aidan and Dre were fully revived. They didn't survive all those centuries by being weak. Near death, they'd almost taken out her consort. She'd also overestimated using them to bait me into killing off the king. We'd forced her hand, but she had an ace up her sleeve and she was prepared to play it.

Four fae guards stepped out of the ether wearing white tunics, a sun embroidered on the chest in gold thread. The line broke off in to two sets of two, each pair pushing huge metal coffins. Instead of the traditional box shape, these were loosely formed in the shape of a man. The head and shoulders were easy to make out. The rest was sort of a cylindrical shape, with no arm or leg definition.

Two sets of hinges ran down each side, the seam for the doors barely visible. The only opening in the entire contraption was an eye slit. Both were occupied. I had no doubt about who was trapped inside the torture boxes. From a distance, I couldn't tell which was Mason and which was my father. As the personal-sized metal prisons were wheeled closer to the queen, I felt the iron. So much of it that my bones ached just being near it. Conry whimpered, backing away from the deadly metal. I possessed the one weapon known to exist that could kill a fae.

The queen made another.

"I'm sure you've heard of the iron maiden? A unique torture device made by mortals during medieval times. My blacksmiths have perfected it. There were losses, as I'm sure you can imagine, working with iron. With progress comes casualties." Tianna walked to where the guards stopped several feet away, gesturing to the two chambers like one of those Price Is Right girls.

"How long have you kept them in there?" There was no right answer to my question. Even a few hours trapped inside that much iron would weaken them. It had been days at home, longer inside Faerie. They'd be close to death by now, drained of their essence. If she triggered the iron maiden, they'd die. "How long?" My voice echoed throughout the Court of Light.

"You will do this for me!" Tianna screamed.

Tick, tick, tick. A timer. And then it stopped. A brief moment of silence. The loud click of metal, followed by the soft wet sound of it forcing its way through flesh was barely audible over the queen's tyrannical laughter. No other sounds, not a cry or whisper, just the pooling of blood beneath the iron cases. And then it hit me. A wave of grief so consuming when it crashed into me it ripped me bare, tore everything from me. Compassion, love, kindness these became words not feelings. I'd been stripped of the knowledge and understanding of those emotions. All that remained, the only things filling the cavity of my body and soul, was pain and rage. Death. I became the hand of death. I would kill everything and everyone responsible for taking Mason and my father from me. Like a plague, I would lay waste to the Court of Light, destroying everything in my path.

I moved, only a few meters separated me from Tianna. I imagined the Retaliator slicing through her skin, found peace in the idea that she would lay dead on the floor from my hand. And then something sparked in my brain. What if the queen was right? What if I could save them and I wasted valuable time killing Tianna? She would still be here if I failed. A glimmer of hope. I'd found a new direction, new purpose.

The veil enveloped me. Conry burst through the grey at the last moment. His ability to channel energy for me was essential. I silently thanked my father for choosing this Cwnn Anfwnn as my guardian and set myself to work. Time is the true measurement for all things, for life. Without time there is no proof we existed at all. I had no idea how to manipulate it, no spells to distort it. So I tried the only thing I knew. I broke down one reality and rebuilt another. The Court of Light where I stood, the two iron maidens with the precious blood, the life of my loved ones pooled on the floor, disappeared. I stood on the precipice of nothing, at one with the Between and the power that allowed me to move through it.

The queen's court began to take shape again. This time, I stood in front of the iron maidens. The tick of the timer the only sound. I'd slowed everything down to match it. Tick. I moved forward. Tick. Tianna yelled, the sound dragged out. Tick. Three left before the gears engaged and the deadly iron pins pierced their flesh. I hit the release switch. Tick. The doors swung open. Mason collapsed in my arms. Tick. Tears streamed down my face. It was easier to hold him than it should have been. He was emaciated, dehydrated, bruised and beaten,but alive. I set him gently on the floor. Tick. My father.

I knew I loved Mason. I realized that months ago, just I'd never managed to tell him. I'd given him everything I could, my body, my time, the best of me. All he wanted was for me to say those three words. I told him actions speak louder than words. I was wrong. Sometimes they need to be heard. So I said them.

"I love you, Mason Hunter." And then I disappeared into the veil again.

I repeated the process, Conry at my side. Deconstructed the reality where I freed Mason and focused on my father. The timer ticked and I synchronized myself with it. Something was different. Something was wrong. The triggers were set to go off at the same time. If I changed this moment it would undo the moment I saved Mason. My heart constricted. Fear of failure and what that meant seized my mind. I froze, unable to change the moment where I saved Mason, unable to leave my father.

Conry funneled energy to me and bolstered my strength. His muzzle nudged my palm and I wrapped my arms around his neck, burrowing my face into his thick, soft coat. Conry wouldn't leave my father here either. Arawn was the leader of the Hunt, the head of his pack, as much a father to him as to me. Conry sat in front of the iron maiden, waiting. Waiting for me to save him.

I tried again. This time I concentrated on going back earlier. There wasn't enough time to save them both in the same moment. With Mason safe, I could go back a few seconds before and free my father. I focused on the instant the queen's guards brought out the torture devices, tried to go back. And then I tried again and again. Every time I failed. I couldn't go beyond the moment I freed Mason. Conry whimpered, scratching at a spot on the floor in front of my father's prison. Exhaustion took over and I dropped down beside him. He curled up next to me, his warmth soaking into my bones and fighting off the chill that set in. We were completely drained of power so I pulled the grey to us, spindled enough of the Between into us both to try again. The results were the same.

I collapsed. Cool marble pressed against every inch of my exposed skin, amplifying the chills. My body had given up. My mind had not. I felt myself flickering like a light bulb about to go out, sort of in this reality and in the Between over and over again until there was nothing left. I solidified on this plane, on the floor next to Mason. Without my father. Without the strength or power to go back again. There was a hole in my chi. I think I broke it because I couldn't spindle energy any more. Tears rolled down my face, silent sobs jerked my body. I didn't save him. Mason's fingers found mine and laced them together. He felt it, as a member of the Wild Hunt, he felt the loss of my father. Conry howled drowning out Amalie's gasp.

"You see,Your Majesty? I told you she could do it." Kellen managed to get his wounds tended to while I was in the Between.

"That's debatable,Consort. She only saved one." Tianna wasn't as impressed with my performance.

"On her first attempt. If she honed the skill..." He trailed off, let that sink in.

"Perhaps. We shall see. If she fails again, you will share the same fate. No one leaves. Take them to the dungeons. Limited rations, be sure that one eats and drinks." The queen pointed at me.

The heel of someone's boots hitting the floor could be heard coming from the furthest side of the room. I assumed it was more guards, come to take us to our cells. And then I heard his voice. Ballard. I almost wept with relief. "What took you so long?" I whispered as he passed by me.

"You've been a busy little bee,Wife." The king's voice boomed, bouncing off the marble walls.

Tianna actually stepped back. "Husband."

"Is that the daughter of Arawn? My, my you have been busy. And is that the Lord of Other World in there?" Ballard tapped the iron maiden, pulling away when he felt the burn of the metal on his fingertip. He shook his head, tsked at his wife.

"My dear, what have you gone and done? Killed poor Arawn? What did he ever do to you?"

"I merely held him captive. She let him die." The queen's words stung. She knew I blamed myself and couldn't resist getting another blow in.

"You've gone too far this time, Tianna. I've overlooked your treachery over the centuries. This, I cannot. Killing the Harbinger in order to force his daughter's hand? To force her to kill me for you? Nay, this I cannot and will not overlook."

"Spies," she hissed. "I will root them out. Rip every one of them from my court."

"The eternity we have been granted would not be enough time to accomplish such a goal." Ballard stepped closer. There was a tenderness in his eyes I did not expect to see. Despite all their flaws, despite her attempt to have him murdered, he loved her.

The queen saw it too and tried to use it to her advantage. "Ballard, my love, let us come to terms. Reconcile ourselves and our courts. We could rule together as in the days of old." Tianna spoke the words he longed to hear.

She slipped a hand in a pocket hidden in the folds of her gossamer gown. The king cocked his head to the side, eying his wife speculatively, scrutinizing her every move. He saw the blade before she fully unsheathed it, blocking the blow when she rushed him. Sadness crept in his eyes for a brief moment and then it was gone. That was all he could afford anymore and her blade would have found a home in his chest. His hand clamped on her wrist, squeezed until she dropped the blade. Ballard spun her around and pinned her arm behind her back in a painful chicken wing position. The Dark Guard came to take her away, placing her in iron cuffs and shackles.

"She truly meant to kill me this time. Undo everything we've created. Watch it all dissolve, slip away like sand through your fingers." He spoke to everyone in the throne room and those lurking outside the columns.

A crowd began to form upon his arrival, curious to see the monstrous dark king their queen loathed so passionately. The soft hush of whispers carried over to us. Most seemed surprised by his good looks and the lack of brutality he'd shown so far. The queen told elaborate tales of the beast he'd become, yet here he stood, handsome and completely lucid. That last part was debatable in my opinion. I'd spent time in his court. The queen's assessment wasn't far off. Not that I'd tell him that.

"The distance between our courts was not enough? Since you wanted so desperately to be rid of me, I think a fitting punishment would be eternity by my side. Where I can keep an eye on you." Ballard gave his wife a little wink as she screamed and railed against the guards that held her. "Our courts will remain as they are. Separate, yet equal." He spoke to the crowd. "We will stay until a new king or queen has been selected from one of your fine houses. The sooner you come to an agreement, the sooner your new king or queen ascends to the throne and the sooner you will be rid of us." He called a

Guard to him. "Go with them, take her to her chamber. The shackles and cuffs remain on. I will join you shortly."

The fae dissipated, running back to their respective houses to determine whose name would be thrown into the hat. Who would lead them? What would become of them? I left it up to the king. I couldn't help them. I couldn't even help my father.

A wave of grief crashed into me, but the tears wouldn't fall. Mason dragged himself closer to me, laid his head in my lap and wrapped an arm around my waist. Too weak to hold me, to cradle me in his against his chest, he offered the next best thing. I ran fingers through his hair with one hand while I stroked Conry with the other. The weight of my friends' sadness pressed against me. I felt them at my back, all three of them huddled together, sharing my heartache and the loss of my father.

"His body and soul has already been returned to the Between." Ballard looked at the iron maiden his wife commissioned, the one that held my father and then back to me. "Your father and I had our quarrels. Most notably over your mother." He paused, a weak half-smile on his face at some memory of the three of them - the king and my parents. "I feel his loss already. I should very much like to tell you about her. About your mother. Perhaps you could join me sometime, as a way to show my gratitude for your warning." So he did get my message. "Alas, that will have to wait for another night.

Before I have you escorted back to Salem, I have a gift to bestow upon you."

"If it's another relic, you can keep it." I had enough of those already.

He snapped his fingers and yet another small cluster of guards came forward. He must have emptied the dark court of its warriors before coming here. One of the men tossed a withered heap on the floor. The body slid to a halt near the king's leather clad feet. I knew who it was before she held her head up to look at me. Mahalia. Blood magic had not been kind to her, taking a physical toll on her every time she used it. Her hair lost its luster. The flowing, white locks she had the last time I'd seen her lost their shine, her brittle mane matted to her scalp and face. She looked every bit the crazed, evil witch she had become. Rot set in at her gum line and began to overtake her teeth. The fetid breath and body odor almost made me gag. She looked and smelled like she hid in a cesspool to evade capture. I suspected it was one of Ballard's dungeons.

"How long have you had her?" How long had I been wasting my time searching for the wretched witch?

"Not long after you accused me of breaking her out. You've been hunted by the Dark Guard. I believe you're familiar with how determined they can be."

He had her before Lawrence? "So if she was imprisoned in the Court of Shadows, who's responsible for the massacre at the Tune and Lube?" Why couldn't it just be her? Why didn't

243

there have to be more of them? More dark witches, another blood coven to shut down.

"I can't do everything for you, Maurin. One can deduce from the level of sacrifice at that particular location that her henchmen were trying to free their priestess. They failed, obviously." Ballard brushed a piece of lint from his sleeve.

He'd already lost interest in us. Well, except for Amalie. Ballard had a witch in his care once. My mother. I'd yet to hear Ballard's version of my mother's time in the dark court - or anyone's version of it for that matter - something told me Amalie wouldn't enjoy falling to the same fate.

Amalie stepped out from her vampire huddle to get a better look at the wretched creature curled up on the floor. Face to face with her mentor, the woman she'd looked up to as high priestess of her coven, the woman who bound her, who betrayed her religion, Amalie crackled with energy. The conflicting emotions added to her magic, making it dangerously unstable.

"So the bonds have been cut." Mahalia's voice cracked, her throat dry from lack of water, probably hoarse from screaming during her stay in the bowels of the dark court. "Oberon is a fool. You are a danger to everyone around you. Ever since you came into your magic, I knew you'd be too weak to control it. You had all the makings of a priestess, but you lacked a hunger, that desire to hold limitless power in your hands, to truly use it. I did you a favor."

"And what of the witches you killed? The ones you led down a dark path? Did you do them a favor, too?" Amalie spat the words at Mahalia. Now that the evil festering inside the old crone was visible on the outside Amalie was finally able to see Mahalia for what she was.

"A means to an end. They fulfilled their purpose." Even after she was captured, Mahalia refused to believe she was wrong, that what she'd done was wrong.

Amalie heard enough. Her hair floated around her, clothes rippled in a wind no one else could feel. Energy surrounded her. Her eyes closed, Amalie took a deep breath and began muttering words in Latin.

Mahalia laughed it off, the sound phlegmy and ragged. "That spell hasn't been performed in centuries, since the last of the inquisitions in Europe. You mean to bind me?"

"Like the witches of old. Just like you did to me." Amalie continued without missing a beat.

Small cords of light in varying colors wrapped around Mahalia's body only to be absorbed and new ones formed in their place. Layer after layer of the spell settled into her skin, her soul. You could see the magic, what was left of Mahalia's power being snuffed out. Without her magic, the years caught up with her. Age spots appeared on her hands and face, wrinkles deepened and multiplied. She'd essentially become a Norm.

The king seemed familiar with the spell Amalie used, probably because it belonged to the fae. Ballard watched her, intrigued by the power she wielded. He analyzed the magic, examined the differences from fae magic and seemed to approve. She'd captured his attention. I wasn't sure if that was a good thing.

"Maurin, I believe you promised justice with the tip of your sword." Ballard encouraged me to unsheathe the Retaliator and finish her off.

Exhausted emotionally and physically, I'd lost my taste for blood. I just wanted to take Mason home and lay my father to rest. "I think living out her remaining years like this in your dungeons would be a much better ending to her story. If you can keep her there, that is."

"You won't have the same problems with my jailer. It's been a long time since he's had someone to play with. He'd grown quite fond of this one." Ballard gave a little wink as the second woman was dragged from the great room.

Blood and filth marred the beautiful white marble floors. Darkness touched the Court of Light. It wasn't Ballard's doing. The queen became what she feared would happen to her people if the Court of Shadows remained. She blackened her aura, tainted her soul all on her own. I hoped the fae that pledged fealty to her crown, her most loyal supporters, realized that and didn't try to take up the queen's cause.

Kellen slunk away, hoping no one would notice his escape. We'd been distracted by Mahalia, it was the perfect time to get away. But there was one guard he would not evade. Elowyn. I'd been on the receiving end of her fist and no doubt her bow. If for no other reason than to avoid her, I planned to stay on Ballard's good side. She stepped out from behind one of the massive columns. Her arm drawn back, bow tight, she released an iron tipped arrow. It sank into his skull with a dull thud. Kellen remained upright for a moment, as if nothing happened. And then his legs, no longer under the control of his brain, buckled. He crumpled under the weight of his own body like someone balled up a piece of loose leaf paper.

Elowyn lowered her bow, slinging it over one shoulder and across her chest. She shrugged her shoulders, her commander's raised eyebrows. "He was trying to escape, Cirian."

Tired of the struggle to restrain his second in command, Cirian took an opportunity to chastise her in front of the King. "Your liege has not given an execution order. You would do well to remember whom you serve, Elowyn."

Exasperated, she sighed and threw up her hands. "It's not enough iron to kill him."

"No, just enough to render him useless. The iron will fester in his brain, stealing his ability to think or act for himself. You might as well have killed him. Now he will be someone's burden to care for eternity. Perhaps yours?" Cirian seemed more upset about the result of Elowyn's actions than the actions themselves.

"His brother shall care for him. A reminder to his family and his house of what happens when you make unwise allegiances. Now, if the two of you are finished, please escort our guests out of Faerie." Ballard turned his back, our cue it was time to go.

21

The sun remained safely below the horizon when we jumped through the Between. We decided on Mason's apartment, centrally located between Amalie's and Risqué. This would be the first of many nights I'd stay at Mason's place. I looked at the clock on the cable box. Less than an hour passed this side of Faerie, plenty of time to get the vampires back to the club and tucked safely underground while they finished healing. Aidan made a quick call to Agrona while Amalie helped me get Mason into the bedroom. Still weak from the iron, he had a hard time walking on his own. He needed a shower as much as he needed the sleep, but that could wait until he could carry his own weight to the bathroom.

"I'm going to go call Oberon, see if he can pick me up." Amalie rested a hand on my shoulder, giving a little squeeze.

"I'll be out in a minute. I just..." My voice broke. I closed my eyes and took a deep breath to stop the flood of emotions from washing me away.

"Take your time. I'll let the guys know you'll be out in a few minutes. We won't leave without saying goodbye."

I stood at the edge of the bed looking down at my strong, beautiful man covered in bruises, dirt and dried blood. I managed to save him, to shift not only reality, but time. I felt relieved that he lived, immense joy that he would recover and we'd be together, grief and guilt tainted all of that.

Kellen's words played over and over in my head, "If she honed the skill". Did that mean I could do it again? Could I go back further and save my father? Or would that undo saving Mason? Was I destined to only have one of them in my life? Ill fated, that's what Kellen called half-bloods like me. He was right. That didn't mean I wouldn't try to bring my father back.

"Stop it. I know what you're thinking." Mason's hoarse voice barely above a whisper. "I know you, Maurin Kincaide, daughter of Arawn. It can't be done."

"Shhssshh." I sat on the mattress beside him, careful not to jostle him too much. "You need to rest. Everyone is leaving. I'm going to see them out and then I'll make you some tea with honey for your throat okay?" He managed to raise a hand to cup my face so I turned my head just enough to kiss his palm. "Rest. I'll be back in a few minutes."

His eyes closed and breathing relaxed. A soft snore rumbled out as I kissed his forehead. I left him in his room, pausing to check he was still there and this wasn't a dream when I reached the doorway. With Mason safe in his bed, I joined the others in the kitchen clustered around the table.

"You're an angel, you know that?" I took the cup of fresh coffee from Amalie, reveling in the rich flavor and warmth.

"I made a full pot. Oberon is outside. You'll probably be asked to appear before the coven. Or at the very least meet with Oberon. He wants to see your reports for the Council on the blood covens and Mahalia. I have access to those. I'd expect a follow up call for sure." Amalie rinsed out her mug and set it in the sink. "If you need anything, Maurin, call me. I mean it, even if it's just to talk. I know Mason heals fast, but he was exposed to so much iron. I can whip up some charms at home if he needs them. Or some of my special chamomile tea if you have trouble sleeping." She didn't mention my father. She didn't have to. I knew she shared my pain. Amalie lost her parents too and knew all too well no amount of "I'm sorry for your loss" will make it better. She saw herself out after giving me a hug and kissing Aidan and Dre on the cheek.

"Be sure to look after yourself while you're looking after him. Otherwise, this one will be over here every night making sure of it." Dre nodded in Aidan's direction. He pulled the pipe I bought him for Christmas out of his coat, packed it with tobacco, then dug the box of matches out of his pocket, giving it a little shake to make sure it wasn't empty. "I need a smoke, think I'll wait for our ride outside. Maurin, I... I'm so... what I mean to say is..... Mind if I drop in on you two sometime this week?"

Relieved he spared me the words I knew he meant, but really didn't want to hear, I drained my coffee cup. "Of course not. You're always welcome here. Although, I doubt the Council will give me more than a day or two off." I smiled, setting my mug on the counter before walking him out. The fae blood went a long way to healing Dre and Aidan,but based on his stiff movements they still had a long way to go.

"We called over to the club. They're sending a car. Agrona agreed to be our hostess for the next few days until we've fully recovered. She wants to inspect our injuries. Seems she thinks our little witch was right and we lacked the conviction to prevent a magical attack. Should be a fun way to spend the hours before sunrise." Aidan stood a few feet behind me, to the left of the couch.

A few years older than Dre, Aidan healed at a faster rate. His feet were light, managing to sneak up on me where as Dre shuffled his way to the door. I turned around, taking stock of what injuries remained. His clothes looked worse than he did.

"Thank you. For helping me, for helping him."

"I only wish there was more we could have done. I fear we let you down in the end. Your father..."

"Don't, Aidan. Don't say he'd be proud of me or how much he loved me. Not right now, not tonight. I can't, okay? I just can't." Tears threatened to fall again, burning my eyes as I fought to hold them back. A dam did not exist that could hold back the tears when he pulled me into his arms.

"You are going to have to come to terms with this loss, face the pain. Burying the grief like you do every other emotion besides anger isn't going to fix it. I have seen my share of loss over the years, watched two generations of my family, all of the births and all of the burials. You know that I'm here for you."

The problem with admitting I had someone to grieve - it meant admitting I lost someone. And in my mind, I hadn't. Not completely, not yet, anyway. There was a chance, however minuscule, and I held onto it with every fiber of my being.

Feet shuffled behind us. I peaked around Aidan to see Mason leaning on the wall in the hallway leading to his bedroom. I unwrapped myself from Aidan's arms, wiping the tears away. "What are you doing up?" I rushed over to him.

"I'll leave you to it." Aidan nodded at Mason. "Glad to see you're alright."

"Thanks again, Aidan." I slung Mason's arm around my neck to help him back to bed.

"No need to thank me, my dear. We have an arrangement. I fully expect you to hold up your end of the deal." With a wink and a small bow, Aidan headed outside to wait with Dre for their ride.

"What deal? What did you do, Maurin?" Mason whispered, suffering from full blown laryngitis.

"Nothing, it's no big deal." I stumbled a little under his weight. "Sorry."

"The fact that you said it's no big deal means it is, in fact, a big deal." He managed a smile even though I knew he worried about what I might have done. I felt the tension in his body.

"Not this time. I swear. Now, what are you doing out of bed?"

"I had this smoking hot nurse. Did you see where she ran off to? She disappeared on me."

"Smoking hot, huh? Well this nurse says you need to get back in bed and no talking."

"I can think of a few things we can do in bed that require no talking."

"You're incorrigible, you know that? I'll be sure to let Amalie know you don't need any of her healing amulets." I helped him down onto the bed.

He grabbed my hand. "Stay with me tonight. Please."

"I'm not going anywhere. Except to the bathroom to get a hot face cloth to clean you up a little."

He relaxed, his shoulders dropping a notch. "This is what a guy's gotta do to get you to spend the night?"

"No, just to make me realize that I'm hopelessly in love with you and plan on spending every night here." That little admission got him to stop talking. "It helps that your apartment is way nicer than mine.

I went to the bathroom and came back out with the hot towel and a glass of cold water from the sink. It wasn't the tea I'd promised,but it was wet and we'd be curled up together under the covers that much faster if I wasn't making tea. Once I'd cleaned him up, a job both of us enjoyed more than we should have, given the serious nature of his injuries, I tucked us both in and turned on a James Bond marathon.

Mason rolled over on his back, letting me snuggle in with my head on his chest so I could see Goldfinger. "I always had a thing for Money Penny."

"Really? Not the sexy damsel in distress or the dangerous vixen?" I looked up at him, thankful for the light banter, some semblance of normalcy.

"Nah, too much work. Besides, Money Penny *is* sexy. She's smart and confident, gives as good as she gets with James. Reminds me of someone." He kissed the top of my head.

"Really? Who is she? Should I be worried?"

"Very." He managed to keep a straight face long enough for my head to pop up. "She finally told me she loves me. Things are getting serious."

I propped up on one elbow, stretching so I could close the distance between our mouths. He raised himself up, only wincing once, to meet me. When our lips touched, the soft moan that escaped him wasn't from pain. I deepened the kiss, pouring everything I felt for him into it. His hands roamed my body, kneading, squeezing every inch he could reach before sliding me on top of him. I straddled him, his hands on my ass pressing me against him, never once breaking the kiss. He winced a few times, flinched from the pain when my weight settled on a tender spot. He didn't stop. He needed it, wanted it as much as I did.

He almost died, and that would have been reason enough to want this, to push through experiencing pain to the point of ecstasy. I'd told him I loved him when he was barely conscious lying on the floor in the Court of Light. Mason needed this, needed to feel our bodies skin to skin, as close as two people could be, joined body and soul. I needed to forget about death, the trappings of mortality. I needed to feel loved, to feel alive.

The rush of passion dulled the pain, fueled his desire, and bolstered his strength. He rolled us until he was on top, slowly and methodically moving his hips, taking me to the edge again and again, but never over it. His hands were entwined with mine, stretching our arms above our heads.

He rocked his hips, burying himself inside me, hitting the spot that made me come undone. "I need you, Maurin. Be my mate. Marry me." His breathing increased, voice husky as he joined me in climax.

"Yes, yes." The words fell from my mouth before his lips captured mine again.

We watched the rest of the marathon cuddled up, dozing on and off.

"When you're ready, I want to show you how to connect with your father in the Between. I'm not going to rush you or pressure you. Just hold you up, keep you from drowning. As much or as little as you can take."

I nodded, my head still on his chest. I didn't want to connect with my father in the Between. I simply wanted my father. Was it too much to ask? Why give him to me in the first place, only to rip him away so soon? If I told Mason my plans to hone the skill, to master it like Kellen seemed to think I could, I'd just ruin what was quite possibly the most perfect moment of my life.

He asked and I said yes. That was enough for one night.

I woke still tucked into Mason's side, his arm draped across me out of bed, daylight peaked through the blinds. Exactly as I imagined, the smell of fresh bread and baked goods wafted up from the bakery below. I saw a scandalous affair in my future with a cinnamon bun, cheating not just on Mason, but my beloved croissant as well. In desperate need of some sweet calories, I slipped out from under Mason's unbelievably heavy arm and threw on my clothes.

Undeterred by my disheveled appearance I made my way down to the bakery. The line ended at the entrance to the alleyway leading to the apartment. It looked like everyone else in Salem came up with the same idea. By the time I got inside, there were two hot crossed buns, one banana chocolate chip muffin, one square of cinnamon crumb coffee cake and one low fat raisin bran muffin. I settled on the banana muffin and the coffee cake because let's be real, hot crossed buns is simply fruit cake pretending to be a cinnamon bun. I placed my order, adding two dirty chai lattes to the total.

I crept back in to the apartment, careful not to wake Mason, only to find him sitting up in bed with the sheet seductively pooled around his waist.

"You're still here." His smile and genuine surprise said it all. He thought I left.

"Of course I'm still here. I wanted to see what all the fuss over this bakery was about. Banana chocolate chip muffin or coffee cake?" I held up the white paper bag containing the proffered baked goods.

"What? No cinnamon buns or croissants?"

"Apparently, you have to get up a lot earlier than," I glanced at the clock on his nightstand, "quarter of eight."

"Well, it is Saturday morning." He patted the spot I'd vacated half an hour ago. "So no second thoughts then?"

"No second thoughts. You're stuck with me, Mason Hunter. Unless you want the coffee cake. Then all bets are off."

"Banana chocolate chip muffins are my absolute favorite."

22

A month passed since I gave up my apartment and moved in with Mason. Three weeks since I purchased a marker and had it placed in Greenlawn Cemetery. The Council worked out an agreement with the Preservation Society, allowing a simple flat stone to be placed in an alcove between two of the buttresses on the side of the chapel. The ivy covering the side of the stone walls and stained glass windows which turned a red vibrant enough to rival the autumn leaves long since died away. The landscape barren of any vegetation, untouched by the coming spring, seemed a perfect setting for these visits with my father.

Mason thought it would be good for me to have a place to go, something rooted on this plane to help me focus on my connection to him in the Between. I found it to be the best place to practice shifting time. No one questioned the grieving daughter or my motives for going out to the cemetery so much. I took to talking to him on my visits. The same one-sided conversation happened every time I came, first I apologized for failing to save him and then I promised to make it right. Two to three times a week for the last three weeks I followed the same routine.

I brushed the grass clippings left behind from the grounds keeper off the stone and settled in to try again. I concentrated on the stone at first, switching up to my father's image and finally the moment of his death. I pulled the veil around me, targeting that one moment in time, never physically shifting more than a few seconds back. Like every other day, I repeated the process until exhaustion took hold. I collapsed on the ground, the damp earth setting a chill deep into my bones. Disappointed with my lack of progress I dissected my latest failure.

"You can't keep going like this." Ballard balanced on the balls of his feet atop the buttress, his leather trench coat billowing out behind him. He dropped down next to me, his boots just missing my head. "I never understood why people need these places. The body dies, the soul ascends and so the circle continues."

"It makes people feel better. What are you doing here anyway?" I sat up, my back against the chapel wall.

"And do you feel better coming here?" He looked down at me, crossed his arms over his chest and waited for my answer and ignoring my question.

"Sometimes," I lied. He knew it.

"You'll never be able to go back to that moment. No matter how many times you try, no matter how much of your life you waste sitting in this place or how much energy you spend in the Between, it cannot be undone."

"I did it once," I said, my tone defiant.

"Precisely. You changed that moment already. You made a choice."

"I didn't choose Mason over my father." I stood up, pushing off the wall, eager to get some distance between me and the king of shadows.

"I never said you did. Just that you made a choice to actually change time. Is that what you think? That you chose one over the other?"

I didn't answer. I never stopped to think about it beyond my father's death and that I wanted to save him. Still, the question begged to be answered. Ballard took my silence as a resounding yes. I suppose I did, too. I resented not being allowed to have them both, that my father died so soon after our reunion.

"What if you could do that moment again? Knowing what you know now, that you could only save one of them, would you choose your father?"

"Well maybe if you showed up sooner I wouldn't have had to choose."

"That took longer than I expected. Most people would choose to blame someone else before bearing the burden themselves. You are a complicated woman. I needed to know if you were capable of doing what Tianna said. It has never been done before, not by anyone. Not even your mother. You are known for doing the impossible. I couldn't risk the existence of my people. I had to know because as much as it would have pained me to deny the world a creature such as yourself, I would have killed you. It is time to give up this exercise in futility."

"I want to have them both." I spun around, throwing my hands in the air. "Is that so wrong?"

"Of course not, but there's a cost for tampering with time. Even a millisecond. Arawn paid the price for you. He foresaw that precise moment. He made a choice so that you wouldn't have to. The Harbinger allowed himself to be taken. And he would have done it again and again. For your future, for your happiness, he would have done anything. And both of those things lie in the hands of the man walking towards us."

"Did you, does he know what I've been doing?" I watched Mason cross the cemetery with a determined stride.

"I've said nothing. I can tell you that he suspects something. He did not become the hunter by being a foolish man. He's been waiting for you to come to him for help, to ask him why no matter what you do you get the same results. Some people might say that is the definition of insanity, you know. Not me of course, but some people."

Mason exchanged a head nod with the king in way of greeting. "Ballard."

"Huntsman. I think I shall take my leave." The king tugged at his coat. "Oh, there is one more thing. The real reason for my visit. The Wild Hunt is a man, or in this case, a woman short. It cannot ride without someone to lead them."

"Mason will lead them. He's the obvious choice." I wanted to follow up with "duh", but decided against it.

"He is not in the line of succession. If you wish to appoint another that is your right. Other World has been absorbed by my court where it splintered from so long ago. However, the duty of the hunt still falls to you, Daughter of Arawn. You've unwittingly been preparing for this moment all your life. Think hard before making a decision. Should you wish to learn more about your mother, my offer still stands." Ballard faded away as quickly and quietly as he arrived.

"You ready to come home?" Mason really wanted to ask if I was done.

I answered both questions, spoken and unspoken. "Yes."

He pulled me into a hug, kissing the top of my head. "We can stop at Brewed Awakening on the way."

"I'm allowed back in the Grind." The coven lifted my unofficial ban from my favorite coffee shop once I presented the evidence of Mahalia's guilt in the blood coven case during their last meeting.

"Daily Grind it is. You've got a lot of offers lately. I'm going to have to put a ring on that finger, make it official, keep the other suitors at bay."

"Maybe you should just carry a stick to beat them back with." I let him lead me away from the sanctuary I'd made outside of the chapel. "Mason?"

"Yeah?" He held my hand, locking our fingers together.

"Do you want to lead the hunt?"

"I never aspired to take your father's place."

"I guess what I'm really asking is will you?"

"Until you're ready."

"What if I never am?"

"You will be, Maurin. It's always been your birthright. One day you will be."

"And until then?"

"I'll help you. Just like I'll help you long after you are. Because I love you, Maurin Kincaide."

"I love you, too, Mas."

About the author:

Dear Reader,

I hope you enjoyed reading Ill Fated. I love hearing from readers. Your feedback is extremely important to me, so please leave a review on the site where you purchased this book.

Want to know more about new releases, events, contests and give-aways? Be sure to check out my Facebook page www.facebook.com/TheMaurinKincaideSeries. It's a great way to keep in touch and I try to interact as often as I can on the page.

Thank you so much for your continued support.
Rachel

Books By Rachel Rawlings

The Maurin Kincaide Series
The Morrigna
Witch Hunt
Wolfsbane
Blood Bath
Mistletoe Meltdown

Coming Soon

Payable On Death, a Jax Rhoades novel
A Haunted Life
It's All Death To Me

www.rachelrawlings.com
twitter: @rachelsbooks
www.facebook.com/TheMaurinKincaideSeries
www.tsu.com/rachelsbooks
www.hallowread.com
www.facebook.com/hallowread